I0618652

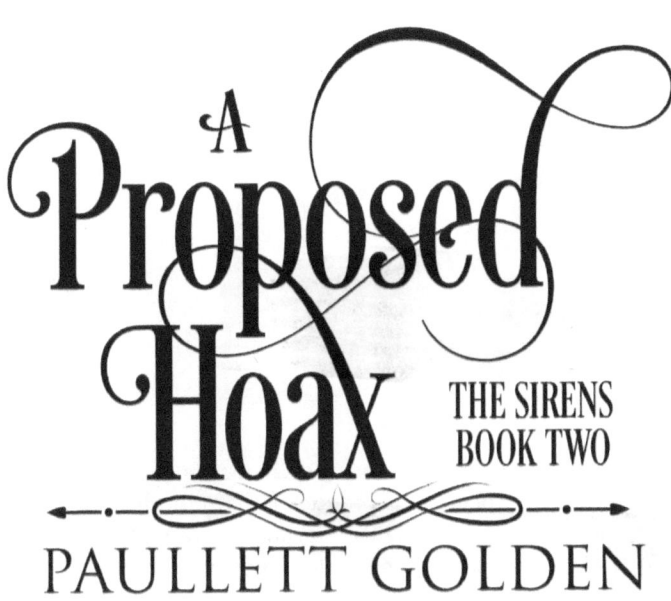

A
Proposed
Hoax

THE SIRENS
BOOK TWO

PAULLETT GOLDEN

Cover Design by Kseniia Pirovskikh
Interior Design by The Deliberate Page

Also by Paullett Golden

This book is dedicated to all who have found themselves standing at the edge of an unexpected change and stepped forward anyway.

Praise for Golden's Books

"The author adds a few extra ingredients to the romantic formula, with pleasing results. An engaging and unconventional love story."

— *Kirkus Reviews*

"Character development is wonderful, and it is interesting to follow two young people as they defy the odds to be together. Paullett Golden's novel is compelling and a stellar work that is skillfully crafted. …easily ranks as one of the best historical romances I have read in some time and I highly recommend it to fans of romance, history, and the regency era. Fabulous reading!"

—Sheri Hoyte of *Reader Views*

"One of the best historical romances I have ever read. Everything about this book is empowering and heart touching."

— *SR.EE Vine Voice*

"There are rare occasions when a plot, characters, dialogue, and backdrop align to make an inspiring book. This is one of those times. This book was a tumultuous, all-encompassing love story. I fell in love with every aspect of this book... The author created a world that I want to visit again and again."

—Jenna of *Reading Rebel Reviews*

"What I loved about the author was her knowledge of the era! Her descriptions are fresh and rich. Her writing is strong and emotionally driven. An author to follow."

—*It Was Only a Kiss* author Shannon Gilmore

"I enjoy the way Golden smartly sprinkles wit and satire throughout her story to highlight the absurdity of the British comedy of manners."

—*Goodreads Reader*

"The author Paullett Golden has a gift for creating memorable characters that have depth."

—Paige Lovitt of *Reader Views*

"An amazing book by an author that has honed her craft to perfection, this story had me gasping with laughter and moping my eyes as the tears rolled down my face."

—*Goodreads Reader*

Chapter 1

July 1796, Shropshire

The village of Tansy Hollow passed in a blink, not because the hired chaise was traveling particularly fast but because the village offered little beyond a church, bakery, and row of terraces. Later, she hoped to find a reason to explore. If all went as she expected, as she *needed*, this would soon become her home.

Her attention shifted to the man on horseback.

With a touch to the brim of his cocked hat, the outrider met her stare. "Twenty minutes, Miss Whittington," he promised over the carriage groans.

She leaned back and tugged at her gloves to avoid her maid's anxious gaze. What said lady's maid did not know was that the outrider accompanied them not for protection so much as to ensure Phoebe did not escape. Again.

This time, she had no intention of diverting course. As far as she was concerned, the sooner they arrived at Lobelia Hall, the better. Then, she would be that much closer to marrying the earl and becoming the Countess of Collumby. Oh, she did not covet the title or the husband who came with it. What this marriage meant was independence from her father and freedom from her past transgressions. It also closed the curtain, with great finality, on that fairytale fantasy called *love*, a play in three acts she was altogether too familiar with and hoped never to attend again.

"I've never been to Shropshire," she said aloud, restless.

Startled, her maid stared wide-eyed at her mistress, obviously uncertain as to what to say or if anything ought to be said.

"I've been to Gretna Green, or very nearly there," Phoebe added, losing her battle against the onslaught of unpleasant memories, "but never to Shropshire."

The maid asked, "You met his lordship in London, then?"

"No, Fanny, I've never met the Earl of Collumby."

"But…"

But indeed.

Phoebe answered the unfinished question with silence, her thoughts on the earl's most recent letter to her father, one of renewed interest. It was an invitation that set her heart racing, not with romance, but with relief: her future might yet be secured.

With each tug of her gloves' fingertips, her heart pitter-pattered. With this one chance to right her wrongs, her only chance, she swore to be on her best behavior, to make certain the earl remained pleased with his decision to take her into his home. She dared not think of the consequences otherwise.

Then, there was no need to fret, was there? She *knew* he would love her at first sight. He had to.

Without cause, she began to laugh aloud, giddy over the weight of matrimony.

Lest Fanny think her mad, she said, "The least amount of effort on my part should win his affection, don't you think? After all, I'm *me*, and he's... well, he's *him*. Hardly fair, really. The only challenge is should he take one look at me and be so pleased, he falls over dead."

Fanny's upper lip twitched. "At least he'd die with a smile."

Phoebe laughed harder. She had to. The laughter hid her deepest fears, for the earl was her only hope.

So intent on rehearsing her only asset — her *beauty* and how best to wield it — she missed the entrance gates entirely. The chaise slowed with a grind of its wheels on gravel as it circled a large fountain, the latter spraying a little too merrily for her mood, then rocked to a stop before the grand E-shaped façade of Lobelia Hall. She swallowed. If so much were not at stake...

With a tilt of her chin, she masked her fears behind a veil of expectation.

The carriage door swung open, and she accepted the proffered hand to step down. Feet firm, she pressed her palm to her fluttering stomach and looked about her. No one to greet her? No servants? No master? They knew to expect her. Where was her welcome?

Her smile quivered. Oh, not from *nerves*, she tried to convince herself, not from a terrible sense of *foreboding*, but rather from the sheer rudeness of being kept waiting.

But what if...

What if her reply had not reached the earl in time? Impatience had urged her to travel the moment her father received the earl's letter. Despite her father's insistence to wait for the earl to offer his own carriage, she had pressed him to dispatch her nearly the next day. Had she been too hasty?

Or worse, what if...

Phoebe blanched.

What if he had already married?

Nonsense. It had taken her only days to reach Shropshire. If he had not married in the year since his first proposal, he would hardly have rushed to the altar so soon after offering her a second invitation. In truth, what young bride would take his intentions seriously other than her? No, Phoebe was unnecessarily fraught. Confidence was needed here. Always confidence.

She brightened her smile with dimples and fluttered her lashes towards the door—half flourish, for the benefit of any eyes that might peer from behind the mullioned windows, and half defense against the dust of the drive—long at last here to meet her betrothed.

The outrider rapped the doorknocker.

The thud echoed, swallowed by silence.

Phoebe curled and uncurled her toes in her slippers, heat prickling at the back of her neck.

They waited.

Too long.

Far too long.

The dry taste of dust and disillusion stuck in her throat.

At last, the hinges creaked as the great wooden door opened. A murmur of voices, the hushed exchange between footman and outrider. Phoebe leaned forward, *expectant*.

A shadow stirred, and then a man emerged.

Phoebe's breath hitched, and then… oh, only the butler.

The butler.

In black livery.

Her smile faltered. Black. The color of mourning. Her world tilted as she swooned.

Phoebe's eyes fluttered open. Soft afternoon light streamed through the windows, dust motes sparkling. For a dizzying moment, she did not know where she was. As disconcerting, she wished she had remained ignorant. Reality flooded back on the scent of lavender salts.

Muffled voices waved in and out of focus until, with the second whiff, every sensation sharpened. She jerked to escape the smelling salts, regretting the movement when a throb of pain pulsed along her leg, presumably where she had landed in her crumple on the drive. Not her finest first impression, to be sure.

Hovering over her, and in crisp focus, was the housekeeper. "There you are," the straight-browed woman said.

Rather than help Phoebe right herself, she stepped back, whispering something to the butler.

Phoebe sat up, gingerly, wincing each inch. A sweep of the room answered her two most pressing questions. She was in the drawing room, and the only inhabitants were she, her ever-anxious lady's maid, the housekeeper, and the butler. Ah, yes, the butler, sporting his mourning attire. As did the housekeeper. Whether the heat behind her eyes was anger that the earl had not waited at least another week before kicking off this mortal coil, long enough to exchange vows, or if the heat was the welling of tears to realize all was lost, she did not wish to explore in front of strangers.

The housekeeper offered, "We are *most* grateful you did not fall upon the marble."

Phoebe pressed a tender hand to her leg. "I prefer rugs for my collapses. They are more forgiving."

In answer, the housekeeper nodded with approval.

The butler bent with the stiffness of age, voice barely above a hush. "We understand you came to call on the late earl. Might we ask your purpose, madam? Perhaps we may be of assistance."

With a slight angle of her head, she declared, as though it were explanation enough, "I'm Phoebe Whittington."

If she expected, which she did, their expressions to light with recognition, perhaps a subtle tug at the forelock to meet their *almost*-countess, she was mistaken. The two exchanged glances and looked back at her in confusion. They were too polite to say as much.

"I am his... I *was* his... I... I was invited by the Earl of Collumby to... discuss a delicate and personal matter. He and my father exchanged letters. I was expected."

Surely, the earl had spoken of her, had prepared his staff for her arrival.

The stretch of silence and perplexed expressions said otherwise.

Right, then. So, this was the end. Back to London. No opportunity, no alternative, no chance to reorient herself or plan anew.

Another exchange of glances, unreadable, before the housekeeper spoke again. "The journey from London is no small one. If it would ease you, madam, the hall may offer you a chamber. At least for the night. Mr. Ellison, the clerk, will wish to attend you regarding the late earl's affairs."

"Thank you," Phoebe replied, her smile fixed though her stomach roiled. "I accept."

Although what she was to say to the clerk was beyond her faculties at present. She could not very well blurt out she was the earl's *almost*-betrothed. What would it serve? All was finished. *She* was finished. London waited, with its whispers and disgrace. Unless… unless the clerk proved useful. And with that fraction of a thought, she renewed hope, or delayed defeat, rather, for here was an *opening*.

Chapter 2

Tugging absently at the glove tips, Phoebe freed her fingers. The guest chamber's tasteful opulence distracted her, however briefly. It evidenced an owner who prized refinement. She wished she had met the Earl of Collumby, if only once. Yet perhaps it was better that she had not.

The tears that stung, however, were not for him so much as for herself. She *did* mourn him, but more so, the hope he had represented. She knew so little about him: a widower four times over, determined to cheat his presumptive heir from succeeding him by taking another bride, a young bride. Beyond that— distinguished or decrepit, kind or cruel—she would never know.

Phoebe laid the gloves in her lap and swallowed the ache rising in her throat. *What was to become of her now?* She would not go lightly back to London. To return meant facing her father's wrath. He had granted her this one reprieve, one chance to redeem herself. Fail, and he would ship her to Calcutta to marry Mr. Darius Vavara, a textile magnate with coffers as deep as his jowls. The ultimatum echoed too loudly: *marry the earl, or I'll send you to India, girl, and let Mr. Vavara make a wife of you.*

She shivered.

Better spinsterhood than that. Alas, spinsterhood was not an option. Her father would see to that.

A faint rustling from the adjoining room caught her attention. "Fanny? Is that you?"

The door to the dressing room angled ajar, and the lady's maid's head of curls appeared in the gap. "Yes, miss. I'm unpacking."

With a snort, Phoebe said, "We've only been invited for one night. What's there to unpack?"

Stepping into the room, Fanny dithered, wringing her hands. "You'll be fine, miss. You always land on your feet."

"Do I?" Phoebe stared at her gloves, wanting to believe her, but then, what did Fanny know? She had only been her lady's maid for a few weeks. "Today I landed on my hip."

Unperturbed, Fanny approached. "Shall I fetch tea? Or see if the laundress has black dye for your muslins?"

"For a singular meeting with a clerk? Would be a waste of both dye and gown. Unless I can find a way to extend our stay, there's no cause."

Phoebe tossed the gloves aside and crossed the room to sit at the poudreuse, only wincing twice as her leg smarted. The mirror was draped in black; lavender sachets reeking of sympathy hung to either side. She stared at the fabric, despondent. If she had married the earl before his breath failed him, all this might have been hers. Instead, she sat like an interloper in a borrowed chair, sorrow for company.

Slipping her feet free, she curled her stockinged toes into the plush rug, the threads thick enough to drown her despair. The dark wood of the poudreuse gleamed. The chinoiserie paper-hangings behind the dressing table tantalized with a floral motif. It was new. And exquisite. Far too handsome for a girl perched on ruin.

Behind her, Fanny crept closer, fidgeting, fussing, and finally sinking her hands into Phoebe's hair to remove the pins and fiddle with the loose curls, ringlets the maid had painstakingly twirled with hot tongs that morning in anticipation of meeting the earl.

Fanny said, far chipper than she should be, "A rest will restore your spirits, Miss Whittington. While you recover, I'll request the dye and tea. By the time you wake, your gowns will be ready for an *extended* stay, and the leaves will be ready to steep for a refreshing brew."

Ignoring this, Phoebe said, her words carried on a sigh, "Easy for you to say when you'll not be delivered to Calcutta for the sin of falling in love. Papa will never forgive me."

Although she could not see Fanny's reflection in the mirror, not with the heavy fabric blotting present, past, and future, Phoebe could feel Fanny's soft breath as she made to reply, then reconsidered.

Phoebe laughed harshly. "You've not seen Mr. Vavara, have you? Picture a mountain of wool bales with a ruby on top. That's to be my husband now."

Voice creeping, hesitant, Fanny offered, "He can't be so bad. You were willing to marry the earl, after all. You'd never met him, and he was, if I'm not mistaken, nearing eighty."

"At least the earl had the courtesy to be a widower *before* remarrying, not to mention I doubt he had a proclivity for pinching young ladies where gentlemen ought not pinch. Oh, and let us not forget the keen advantage that *he lived in England*." She emphasized the last, as though the former were of less degree, when in truth, she would have been willing to live anywhere had the bridegroom been worth the destination.

Without love, it was a fate worse than death. The loss of England, of everything familiar, of the Church of England, even of the language she spoke... She could not do it. She could not.

"No, Fanny. There is no redeeming Mr. Vavara. Papa chose him as my punishment, not my salvation. This is Papa's way of proving there are consequences to following one's heart rather than *his* wishes."

Again, Fanny remained silent. A wise choice. Phoebe's words would have cut deeply had the maid responded, deeper still if the response had been more dribbling optimism. The truth was, Phoebe had been her own undoing. She had gone against her father's wishes to follow her heart, naively unaware that other men were as deceptive and manipulative as her father. Rather than restore her dowry to recommend her to suitors, he reigned over her with perpetual punishment. The sting deepened, knowing he was one of the wealthiest merchants in London, a sizable dowry of no consequence to him. But he did not want her to secure a good match. He wanted her to admit he had been right and she wrong, to reap what she had sown.

"You'll find a way, miss." Fanny broke her silence. "If the new earl were here, you would charm him just as easily as the late earl. If—"

"What did you say?" Phoebe's attention perked.

Fanny's fingers stilled in Phoebe's hair as she thought for a moment. "That you could charm the birds from the trees if you wished?"

"No. About the new earl." With a wave of her hand to dismiss both the request for a repeat and Fanny's ministrations, she stood, pivoting to face her maid. "The clerk!"

Fanny stepped back, timid after her mistress's sudden exclamation.

Phoebe walked to the end of the four-poster bed, gripping a carved bedpost, as if the wood might lend her strength. The ache in her chest softened, no longer grief, but the spark of defiance.

"You said it yourself," she went on, words quickening. "The new earl must be coming. Soon. And if he hides behind a clerk, then Mr. Ellison is where I begin. I'm not without my wit, Fanny. I will learn the answers I need from the clerk, and if he proves stubborn, I shall find my salvation in his paperwork. Clerks love their papers, and papers love to whisper. If there's one thing I've learned from being a merchant's daughter, it's that men spill more secrets to their ledgers than to their wives." She flashed a grin, sharp and sudden. "We've hope yet, Fanny. I'll coax every truth about the new earl from the clerk, or charm it, whichever proves swifter."

Phoebe had barely changed out of her traveling gown before being summoned to the study for Mr.

Ellison's appraisal. She refused to be rattled, though it was plain the clerk did not wish a guest to remain beneath an aristocratic roof without interrogation first. Easier, surely, to charm an earl than a clerk. Clerks were, in her experience, calculating fellows, all logic and figures, impervious to fluttering eyelashes. This clerk, unfortunately, was the gatekeeper to her future.

Battle-ready, Phoebe followed a footman through paneled passages to the study adjoining the library. From what little the footman offered for conversation *en route*, Phoebe discerned they were heading for the *old* study in the *old* library, which evidenced there was a *new* study and a *new* library. She almost smirked at the implication: the clerk had been relegated to the dusty tomes, out from underfoot for when the new earl arrived.

Upon entry, her gaze swept the room. Spacious, scented of ink and leather, sparse of furnishings, but its walls crowded with books and ledgers. A cool, late afternoon breeze stirred the curtains. A faint patter of rain tapped at the panes.

A figure moved from the desk to the windows, and one by one, pulled them closed, then thumbed the latch.

Phoebe drew her black shawl tighter over her pale muslin, a flimsy veil of mourning respectability.

"Miss Whittington." He spoke without turning, voice even, business-like, his focus on latching the last window with deliberate care. "The household has informed me of your... unexpected arrival. Might I inquire the nature of your business with the late earl?"

Her chin lifted. "My arrival was not *unexpected*. His lordship invited me."

A pause, then the faintest edge of amusement. "Indeed?"

Heat pricked her cheeks at the doubt in his tone.

Rather than return to the desk, he crossed to a low table with a tea tray. "Unusual times, Miss Whittington, and more unusual circumstances. I am Mr. Ellison, solicitor to the present Earl of Collumby. May I offer you refreshment?"

He removed his spectacles and slipped them into his pocket before pouring. Without them, he was younger than she expected, though the perpetual crease between his brows betrayed hours bent over accounts. He might even be handsome — for a clerk. But Phoebe's head would not be turned again, not by rogue or solicitor.

"Forgive my caution," he said as he passed her a cup. "Now is when all manner of acquaintances call, hoping for favor or inheritance. That you arrived with considerable luggage is... noteworthy."

"As I said, I was invited." Phoebe steadied her saucer, her hands tense. "My father and his lordship exchanged letters this summer. The most recent, received scarcely a week ago, extended a clear invitation to *stay*."

He studied her over the rim of his cup. "Curious, since his lordship died three weeks ago."

The china rattled in her hands. *Three weeks*? Her father had thought nothing of the battered letter's lateness, nor had she, merely a journey of misadventure. An invitation was an invitation, no matter how weather-worn. But three weeks? Good heavens.

The clerk's smirk told her he thought her a fool. Then, his tone had not sounded curious at all, rather it baited her: *Care to try again*, it undertoned.

She steadied her fingers and sat up straighter. "Not so curious given the state of the post these days. I was invited by the Earl of Collumby as his honored guest and have his most recent letter to prove it."

Inclining his head, he said, "My apologies, Miss Whittington, should you think I have mistaken his honored guest for anything less. Forgive, also, my thoroughness. Claims, in such times, are easily made. To what honor do I owe being in the presence of so honored a guest?"

Phoebe bristled. The audacity of this man! She bit her tongue before she said everything she thought of him. Insulting the gatekeeper would do her no favors; he was her only connection to the new earl. All she needed was a foothold in the house, some way to bide her time.

"That is a personal matter, Mr. Ellison, one I do not wish to discuss with anyone except the new Earl of Collumby."

Cool as ink on a page, he said, "The earl is not due to arrive for several weeks, and all who wish an audience with him must first gain my permission."

His mildness sharpened her temper. He was toying with her, as though she were a petitioner at his gate. Very well. She tipped back her head to gaze at him from down the length of her nose. "I was to have been his betrothed."

His teacup paused midway to his lips, then slowly, he lowered it without drinking and set it aside. Brows lifting, the faint crease etching deeper between them, he said in a careful voice, "Whittington. The name is… familiar."

She seized the opening. "My father is known as the Textile King of London." The words came blunt, proud, challenging him to deny her worth, daring him to say she, being a merchant's daughter, was as likely as her lady's maid to have been the *almost*-betrothed of an earl.

Recognition flickered in his eyes, but he betrayed nothing else, merely studied her as though she were another ledger to be balanced, another column to be tested for error. She hoped he recognized the name only as belonging to a wealthy merchant, not as associated with recent scandal.

At last, he said, "Many make claims when an estate changes hands. Proof of this… understanding… is necessary."

"Proof?" She stiffened, defiant rather than defensive. "You would have me carry a contract in my reticule? My word is proof enough."

"Even a word can be tested." His tone was mild, but his gaze — steady, searching — felt like a blade drawn across silk. "You mentioned a letter?"

"Of course. But I do not have it with me."

"Left in London? You now recall it is not, after all, with you."

"On the contrary. It is in my chamber." Phoebe stood abruptly, ignoring the dull ache in her hip, eager for an excuse to escape this infuriating man. "Shall I retrieve it?"

Mr. Ellison rose with a shake of his head, as though filing her answer away in some hidden account. "Tomorrow. For today, I'll not detain you longer." He motioned to take her teacup.

Phoebe hesitated. She wanted to demand respect, to claim more ground, but his composure offered no purchase. With a breath, she said, "Thank you. I appreciate this time to mourn."

"It is not my intention to be impolite, especially when your heart must be wounded." He set her teacup next to his on the tray. "The household must protect the family's honor. Many would claim connection to the late earl for advantage; you understand why I must ask these questions."

"I understand," was all she said.

"By the by, when I make it known to his lordship you desire his confidence, how do you wish me to introduce you?"

"Tell him Phoebe Whittington requests an audience on a matter most delicate."

"*Phoebe* Whittington?" he repeated, stumbling on her given name.

She canted her head in question. Before she could reply, he recovered his surprise and walked her to the study door.

Once she stepped into the antechamber, she realized her pulse was racing. *Only a clerk,* she thought. *And yet I feel as though I've just faced a magistrate.*

Chapter 3

Graeme listened to the receding footfalls as a footman escorted Miss Whittington away from the study. He hesitated at the door. Only a moment. Only until he spied her black shawl draped over the arm of the chair. It must have slipped when she stood.

When he lifted the lacy confection, a waft of neroli clung to it: light, sweet, with a warmth that lingered like sunlight through silk curtains, absurdly out of place in a study of dust and leather. So, she came armed with orange blossoms as well as eyelashes. He almost laughed. The scent surprised him, not what he expected of a merchant's daughter and hardly the choice of a woman in desperate straits. Neroli was a costly fragrance. Was she playing at wealth to dispel suspicion? Then, if she was the daughter of Mr. Whittington...

He rubbed the bridge of his nose where the spectacles had left their mark. The name Whittington meant something. His father's ledgers were full of it. Cotton shipments. Bengal silks. A fortune that had propped up half the London trade houses. If she truly was Whittington's daughter, then she came armed with more than perfume and dimples. And yet, could he believe that the old earl, supercilious relic that he was, would consent to take a merchant's daughter to wife? The same man who had cut his own brother adrift for daring the same sin? The hypocrisy stung.

Perhaps the earl had wanted to salt the family wound, or perhaps he was simply that desperate to deny his great-nephew the inheritance.

Walking back to the desk, Graeme began folding the shawl to tuck into a drawer, its scent lingering in the air.

It would take more than one interview to discover her game, he realized. However confident he was that she was a fortune huntress, he had no evidence, but then it was not necessarily proof he required so much as her acquiescence.

She unsettled him more than he cared to admit, not just because she might be the Miss P.W. he sought, but because she was far too beautiful to be ignored. Was he such a roué to be distracted by a pretty face? Drifting into thought, he worried the shawl's silk beneath his fingertips.

As he placed it into the drawer, cold metal brushed the backs of his fingers. Absently, he retrieved the signet ring from beneath the folds of the shawl and slipped it onto his pinky finger. Graeme rubbed the crest with his thumb. He feared the estate's unentailed fortune going to a philanderer, and he resented the late earl for wanting to punish his presumptive heir for transgressions two generations passed.

Tossing the ring onto the shawl, he closed the drawer with a *thud* echoed by distant thunder.

Miss P.W.

The estate solicitor's voice echoed in his mind: *the codicil leaves nothing in the coffers... hastily scrawled initials will inherit all unentailed wealth... unwise to contest because of public scandal... find Miss P.W. and persuade her to relinquish it freely.*

Graeme had dismissed the codicil as the carelessness of a dying man, that was until Miss Phoebe Whittington swept into the study with her bold eyes and talk of invitations. Coincidence? Or design? He needed time to investigate. His original intention had been only to assess the condition of the estate and hall and the loyalty of the staff before moving his family into residence, not to carry on an extended charade. Miss Whittington, not to mention the codicil, complicated the matter. He needed time.

Whether Phoebe Whittington was a brazen fraud or the very Miss P.W. named in the codicil, one fact was clear: she could not be allowed to leave Lobelia Hall.

Chapter 4

P hoebe had not slept. For all the chamber's comfort, featherbed included, she had tossed and
turned, rehearsing speeches in her head. By
dawn, she had nothing to show but shadows beneath
her eyes. At least her hip no longer hurt, only light
bruising and a residual tenderness where she had
fallen on the gravel.

All night, she worked and reworked possibilities,
from the scenarios she may face with the new earl to
the myriad persuasions she could use on the clerk to
win his loyalty. Only as the hazy glow of daylight
rounded the curtains' edges did her thoughts drift to
the past, to memories and regrets, to Freddy.

With a shake of her head, she dismissed the remnants of those early morning recollections. Letter in
one hand, the other palm clammy with nerves, she followed the footman. This was it. This was her chance
to turn a single night's pity into something longer,
something that might bring her face-to-face with the
new earl.

This would prove Phoebe's most challenging task
yet. True victory would mean not only an extended
stay, but access to the study in hopes of learning

what she could about the new earl without appearing overly curious in her conversations with the solicitor. She needed to tread carefully to win favor today.

"Miss Whittington," Mr. Ellison greeted her, rising from behind the desk. His spectacles flashed with reflected morning light before he tucked them into his pocket. "I trust you are well this morning."

"As well as can be expected." She touched the black ribbon knotted beneath her bosom, a poor substitute for the missing shawl, but at least a gesture.

"Of course." His tone carried the sympathy his words did not. Mirroring yesterday, he motioned to the tea tray as if they were two acquaintances at a polite call.

She could not decide whether she disliked him for being a barrier to her plans or liked him for being a potential advocate for her cause. His good looks, not detracted by spectacles or the black armband of mourning, did not signify, although she could not deny they irritated her. No clerk had the right to be *appealing*, least of all this one.

With a steadier hand than she felt, she laid the folded letter upon the tray. "I have brought the earl's invitation." Then, nonchalantly, she attended to her teacup, spying his response discreetly from beneath her lashes.

Mr. Ellison unfolded the battered page, brows furrowing. "This is barely legible."

"He had dreadful handwriting," Phoebe said, her tone light.

"It is not only the hand to which I refer." He turned the page in demonstration. "Time has not been kind."

Her pulse fluttered, but she forced a shrug. "Clear enough to see his intent."

The letter had not arrived in the best condition, smudged and torn as it was. The extended travel in her care had not helped its case, adding more tears, crumples, and smudges. Nevertheless, it *was* legible. She only now wished she had brought all his letters. At the time, she never would have expected to need to prove anything to anyone. To be fair, she was unsure what purpose they would serve in her current situation, as she did not wish for a stake in the inheritance, only the household's sympathy, at least until she could charm the new earl. Still, she would have felt more at ease under this man's scrutiny if she could prove her case.

He studied the letter longer than she liked before folding it again. "I will keep this for my records, if you permit."

Her throat went dry. Did this mean he believed her? At least enough not to send her packing or dismiss her outright? Heart hammering, she nodded.

Steepling his fingers, he went on, voice even, "The household regrets you are without a host, but you are welcome to remain for several days, time to recover, to take the air in the gardens, to pay your respects at the chapel." He studied her with the same measured and steady attention he had given the letter. "I can attend you on occasion, though most of my hours are consumed by the late earl's papers. My apologies, Miss Whittington."

Relief surged, followed swiftly by panic. A guest left to wander the gardens might as well be exiled. She needed access, to both him and this study. Her gaze darted, flitting to the desk piled with accounts, correspondences, and who knew what else.

There. The answer dropped neatly into her lap. He had handed her the answer himself!

"You look positively buried, Mr. Ellison." She leaned forward, letting the hint of a smile play at her lips. "My father always said half the battle of trade is in the accounts, and I've spent many an hour rescuing him from paper avalanches. Allow me to assist."

One brow arched. "Difficult to imagine Miss Whittington up to her elbows in invoices and shipments."

She held his gaze. "It will distract me from mourning and spare you the tedium of sorting a lifetime's worth of papers. Surely even clerks wish for an extra pair of hands."

He hesitated long enough for her to sense her victory. At last, he said mildly, "Very well. If you are determined." He glanced at the desk. "The garden accounts. You may sort those by date. Nothing perilous, but let us see if your talents extend beyond smiles."

Phoebe tilted her chin, triumphant. "I've a talent for order, and if it spares you a headache, so much the better. I *am* determined to surprise you, and I firmly believe you will find me as capable with papers as with smiles, Mr. Ellison." Deepening her smile for emphasis, coupled with a bashful blush, she added sweetly, "Perhaps more so."

Her heart leapt as she suppressed her triumph behind a sip from her tea. His concession proved she could gain footing with him, and through him, the new earl. More importantly for now, she had secured her place at Lobelia Hall. Time was all she needed, and she had just won it.

When the door clicked shut behind her, Graeme leaned back in his chair and allowed himself the smallest of smiles. If she thought she had maneuvered him, she was mistaken. He had given her nothing more dangerous than string and ribbons. Let her shuffle bills of lading and trivial correspondence; the true accounts and the codicil would remain locked.

His grin extended beyond outmaneuvering her maneuvers. He was victorious! She did not suspect his motives of invitation beyond sympathy. Her offer to help had, then, played right into his hand. Now, he could observe her, test her, question her at leisure. If Miss Whittington was indeed the mysterious P.W. in the codicil, then every hour she spent in the study would bring her one step closer to revealing herself while allowing him the time either to discover the ammunition to contest her claim in court or to persuade her to relinquish the inheritance. And if she was not the P.W. he sought, merely a clever fortune-huntress, well, he had just bound her with her own rope.

Chapter 5

Grey clouds portended rain, dimming the study into deceptive night. Candleflames wavered at every gust from the open windows. Graeme had readied a stack of harmless correspondence for Miss Whittington to organize, enough to keep her occupied without breaching security. He angled his gaze over the edge of his spectacles to spy the mantel clock, counting down until her arrival.

He hoped to write two letters first: one to the estate solicitor, one to his family. Yet his hand strayed again to the codicil. By now, he could recite the words.

Letting the paper fall limp from his hands, he muttered to the empty room, "To Miss P.W., with whom I spent many quiet evenings, even if only in thought, I leave…"

The old earl's last bequest left the unentailed fortune and a small cottage to the mysterious "Miss P.W." It might have been worse. He might have left *everything* unentailed: investments, properties, holdings, artwork, even furnishings. Nevertheless, the document was dangerous. Hastily drafted on his deathbed, signed and witnessed, but maddeningly vague about the identity of "Miss P.W.," it could be challenged. Weathering the public scandal of a court case would be unpleasant, to say the least. Was it better to risk disgrace or watch the fortune vanish into a stranger's hands?

If, as Graeme now suspected, Miss Whittington was "P.W.," the battle would be harder still. She was spirited enough to fight for what she thought she was owed.

If hung in the air with a stale odor.

For all he knew, Miss P.W. was the late earl's favored opera singer or even hunting dog, not a means to extol kindness, but rather to disinherit his only heir from the money since he could not disinherit the family from the entailment. No opera singer had arrived to claim an almost betrothal, though, only a merchant's daughter with bold eyes and talk of invitations.

Graeme slid the codicil back into its drawer, exchanging it for the shawl she had left behind. Setting the shawl aside to return to Miss Whittington, he tucked the codicil to the back of the drawer before locking it securely. If Miss Whittington had volunteered her so-called help in hopes of finding written validation of her inheritance, she would be disappointed. No reason to give the cat claws.

Fresh paper lay before him. Quill to ink, he began his letter to the estate solicitor, currently in London, handling formalities. The man needed to be apprised of Miss Whittington's arrival — before she made herself at home — and Graeme needed to inquire what, if anything, the solicitor knew of her, from claim to claimant.

Time marched steadily on as Graeme moved from one letter to the next, until, startling him out of his meditative writing, the clock struck the hour with officious precision, as if eager to herald the arrival of Miss Whittington herself. Each chime was a reminder of his solitude's end. He tucked his spectacles into his pocket. Just as the clock tolled six, its heartbeat echoing in the study like a summons, footsteps approached the door, on cue.

A gentle knock.

"Come." Graeme smoothed the final fold of his second letter.

The familiar footman entered, ushering in Miss Whittington, this time with her lady's maid hovering close behind. Graeme suppressed a smile. A harmless *clerk* requiring a chaperone. How flattering.

"Welcome." He rose with a nod.

"Good evening, Mr. Ellison," said Miss Whittington, her gaze flicking over him only briefly before skimming the room. It lingered first on the bundles of twine-tied letters burdening the side table, then on the shawl folded neatly upon his desk. She gave no remark on either. Instead, she directed her maid to the low table and chairs where they had previously taken tea. "You may sit there. A pleasant prospect of the gardens will sweeten the tedium of watching us."

The maid obeyed, her hands twisting, her attention darting, as if she half-expected an earl to leap from behind the curtains.

Miss Whittington paused at the window herself, peering out the fog-streaked glass. "Pity. The garden begged for a walk."

He caught the bait in her tone and parried with bland courtesy. "Nothing would please me more than

PAULLETT GOLDEN

to accompany you." After a pause of only one breath, he added, "When the weather permits."

She hummed noncommittally and turned to the side table. Without waiting for an invitation, she took a seat and tugged at the twine binding one of the stacks, glancing at him through her lashes as if daring him to object.

"You've perceived my intention," he said. "Tradesmen's bills, wine accounts, household receipts. They need sorting before being copied into the ledger."

Without protest, she drew said ledger closer, flipping through the pages with apparent indifference, though he suspected she weighed each sheet for overlooked treasure.

Graeme fetched the shawl and set it beside her hand. "You left this behind."

Her lashes swept up, bold as a challenge. "I should have known you'd come to my rescue, gallant knight."

He had a rejoinder ready, something dry enough to cut the sweetness, but her smile unseated it. His tongue was too thick and heavy to move words. For one dangerous instant, he nearly returned the smile. Sheepish to have lost himself, even for a fraction of a second, he drew a chair opposite hers and reached for a second bundle of receipts, the neroli in the air wrapping around him with a taunt.

Better to work at close quarters, he told himself, than shout from the desk. Easier to ask questions, as well, when he knew her attention was occupied. Or so he had planned before his undoing by way of orange blossoms.

Miss Whittington dipped her pen and bent over the ledger, curls brushing her cheek. The faint scrape of nib against paper was the only sound between them, steady as a heartbeat.

Graeme pretended to study a receipt but found his gaze caught on the flex of her hand, the arch of her fingers, then the tilt of her head as she read, then…. He shook his focus. She made even bookkeeping look deliberate, as if she played at elegance for an audience of one.

At length, he braved, "Forgive me, Miss Whittington, but I cannot help finding your… *arrangement* with the late earl rather curious."

Her quill paused, ink blotting the margin. "Do you?" Without looking up, she shrugged one shoulder. "I don't."

The corner of his mouth lifting, he leaned forward and pressed, "You would have been his fifth wife."

Another shrug. "I know." Her quill moved to the inkpot, then hovered. Her lashes lifted as her eyes met his. "But why not ask what you truly want to know, Mr. Ellison?"

He leaned back, arching a brow. "And what would that be?" Despite his calm composure, his pulse quickened.

With a sly, teasing smile, she bent again to her work. "Why a vivacious young lady should pledge herself to an old man. Is she a dreadful title-huntress? Or — gasp — something *worse*?"

Stunned into silence, Graeme's lips parted, but no words followed.

To his relief, she spared him the trouble of finding a reply. "I thought as much. Who wouldn't wish to know why?" She flicked through a bill for chimney sweeps, her movements too brisk to be careless. "It is no great mystery. My father is… shall we say… *exacting*. Lord Collumby had offered for me last year, but I… declined, a decision my father has ensured I regret. When Lord Collumby renewed his invitation, it came as my salvation. Yes, he had wealth and title, but I sought only to secure a future for myself." Lightening her tone, she added, "I would have fulfilled my duty as wife for what years remained to him, and in return, he would have given me freedom from my father."

His brows drew together.

She dropped the bill onto a neat pile and reached for another, as though the explanation were nothing more than another marginal note. Only the lift of her chin betrayed that the words cost her.

Graeme shifted in his chair, more rattled than he wished to reveal. Her candor disarmed him. He had expected coquettish evasions or bold-as-brass lies harmonized with love songs, not bald truth. His suspicions that there was far more to her story held little weight compared to the honesty of her confession.

"So," he said at last, "you weighed the bargain. Your youth in exchange for… security." Silently, he added *and wealth and title, soon to be untethered.* "Remarkably pragmatic, Miss Whittington."

His gaze lingered on her lashes, willing her to look at him, only to be granted an unreadable expression when her eyes finally met his.

"I didn't crave his ring, Mr. Ellison, only his shield." Bending her head once more over the invoices, her quill scratched neat columns.

Graeme found himself watching the curve of her brow rather than the figures on the page, and that unsettled him more than her confession. Each time he took a breath to ask another question, to seek clarification, or to remark on the weather, a glance at her was enough to silence him, enough so that they worked only to the sound of rain patter. In the back of his mind, he thought he ought to close the windows, but he could not tear himself away from her, spellbound as he was.

The mantel clock struck the quarter-hour, sharp and intrusive.

She awarded him a triumphant grin, her hand motioning to the collated stacks and tidy ledger. "You see, Mr. Ellison? I'm far more than pretty smiles and now have proof I'm talented with keeping order."

I beg to differ, he thought, *for you've disordered me.* Schooling his voice to remain unaffected, he said with a polite incline of his head, "So it seems."

Smoothing her gown with unhurried grace, she rose.

Graeme mirrored her, pushing back his chair. "That will do for today."

With a skip to the door, her maid hastening to join her, Miss Whittington offered a cheerful, "Until tomorrow, then."

"Until tomorrow," he echoed mechanically, though what he meant by it, he could not say.

The supper tray sat half-finished on the little table in Phoebe's chamber, steam from the teapot long since faded. Fanny hovered over it, fussing with the napkin.

Phoebe ignored both tray and maid, gaze fixed on the rain-blurred window. A tiny smile tugged at her lips.

"Our clerk," Phoebe said at last, "is not so impenetrable as he thinks." She leaned back on the settee, satisfactorily tallying her victories. "Did you see him stumble, Fanny? One smile, one flutter of my lashes, and he was pudding!"

Fanny, folding the napkin with unnecessary precision, murmured, "If you say so, miss."

Narrowing her eyes, Phoebe turned sharply. "I do say so. He postures, but he has already begun to yield. By tomorrow, he will be ready to sing my praises to the earl."

Fanny's silence was more eloquent than words.

However bright Phoebe's confidence, the maid's hesitation cast a shadow.

With sudden restlessness, Phoebe rose. "Come. Fetch my shawl. I refuse to be shut up in this room all night, however pretty the curtains. A turn about the hall will do."

"What if—"

"What if Mr. Ellison frowns at me for wandering? Then I shall laugh at his consternation! Or what if the housekeeper scolds me? Then I shall look suitably penitent until she softens. I will not be daunted, Fanny, and neither should you. I mean to see more than the same four walls. Is the plan not that I shall be mistress of the house yet? Come."

Fanny obeyed, retrieving the shawl.

Phoebe swept it about her shoulders, the lace edging trailing over her gown. Crossing the chamber with a decisive step, she muttered to herself,

"If I am to belong here, I must try to feel more at home."

They slipped from the east wing unchallenged, ostensibly for a walk, but really to nose about. No one intercepted them. But then, seeing as she was the only guest, there would be no reason for staff to mill around the first floor, at least not through these corridors. Phoebe carried a single taper to light the way. The flame bobbed with each step, catching gilt frames and scattering shadows across the paneling. Storm-light flashed at the windows, but the corridors themselves lay quiet and deserted.

She wondered where Mr. Ellison lodged. Had he been offered a guest suite in the bachelor wing, or was he housed with staff? Oh, now there was a curious thought... *was* he a bachelor? The question had never entered her mind, not that it mattered since she had no designs on the man, only his employer, and since, married or not, he would be charmed into loyalty, at least enough to help her win the new earl.

This was not overconfidence, she told herself. It was hope. The last vestiges of it, in fact. If she did not have confidence, she might as well slip into the dismals now and be done with it.

Without a destination, she meandered, Fanny trailing behind, more shadow than companion. A few errant turns brought them to the family apartments, their doors silent in the flicker of Phoebe's taper. Looking both ways, Phoebe slipped through the first set of doors, more curious than cautious.

Ah, a private parlor.

Yellow paper-hangings, bright and floral, glowed warm in the candlelight. The furnishings were too new, too pristine, to have been much used. The tables were polished to a gleam, the cushions smoothed, all as opulent as her guest chamber, and all as lonely.

"Cheerful." Phoebe ran her fingers along a marble mantel where two figurines of fig-draped maidens offered baskets of berries. Quaint tokens of a man who liked his comforts—and spared no expense.

Through a connecting door lay a salon, its powder-blue walls pale in the wavering light. A space for games and cards, she thought, with enough room for laughter to echo. The old earl, it seemed, had not denied himself diversion. Would his heir share that taste?

"Miss," hissed Fanny. "I think someone's coming."

Phoebe waved her off, drifting to the narrow window. It overlooked the slanted roof of the minstrel's hall, rain coursing down in silver rivulets, a wending waterfall. Lightning flashed, jagged against the horizon.

"Miss," Fanny insisted.

"Oh, do be sensible. No one is coming. Why would they?"

There were more rooms to explore, but Fanny's fidgeting pressed at her nerves. With a huff, Phoebe guided them through a side door, back to the landing—empty, of course—and turned towards the west wing by way of the connecting minstrel gallery. The taper painted the panels with restless shadows.

"Miss, ought we be returning now?"

Phoebe quickened her steps. "You've no sense of adventure," she scolded, half-teasing, half-cross. Then, with a wicked grin, "If I were to present you to a bachelor marquess with a fondness for maids, would you seduce him into marriage?"

Fanny gasped, her expression tumbling from horror to mortified silence.

"Exactly so. No sense of adventure," Phoebe declared, sweeping onward.

As she crossed the gallery, her candlestick flared, a figure stepping into view from the bend ahead. Phoebe's heart jolted, pulse racing with the storm's rhythm. She raised the taper high—

—and the light revealed Mrs. Redshaw, the housekeeper, her severe face caught in amber glow.

Fanny squeaked.

"Oh! Mrs. Redshaw!" Phoebe let out a startled laugh. "Heavens, I mistook you for a ghost!"

Mrs. Redshaw's mouth twitched, though whether with disapproval or amusement, Phoebe could not guess.

"Ghosts do not haunt Lobelia Hall, miss. Not while I draw breath." Her tone was clipped, practical, yet carried an undercurrent of pride, as though she considered herself guardian not just of the household but of its very walls.

Phoebe lowered her taper, smiling. "Then Lobelia Hall could have no better protector."

The housekeeper's gaze softened, just slightly. "A house reflects the character of its master, and the Hall was kept in good order under his lordship. It shall remain so, God willing." Her hands folded before her. "If you wish for a turn about the house, might I suggest the portrait gallery? The storm makes the gardens unfit, but the gallery offers views of the family line, which some find instructive." Mrs. Redshaw paused, then added with a sidelong glance, "And you will find the chapel just beyond, should you care to offer a prayer. The staff gathers there Sundays with-out fail."

"I would never dream of imposing, but…." Phoebe lowered her gaze. "It would mean more than words can express to join this Sunday."

"We would like nothing better." With a nod, Mrs. Redshaw continued on her way before pausing to eye Phoebe over her shoulder. "You'll find the portraits one turn to the right."

And so, she did.

The gallery stretched the length of the house, lit only by the fitful glow of lightning through alcove windows and the warm flicker of her candle. Faces stared down from the walls, all, presumably, belong-ing to Collumbys of centuries past. She paused at each, tilting the flame to study their features.

Fanny muttered from the opposite side, "Not handsome at all, if you ask me."

Phoebe turned, stopping short. Her breath caught.

The portrait loomed life-sized: a young man, hardly older than she, standing triumphant, sword aloft over a slain dragon. She needed no plaque to tell her this was the late Earl of Collumby. Recogni-tion struck her like thunder. She had never met him, never seen his likeness, yet she knew his face with a curious and inexplicable familiarity.

He was nothing like the bent, gnarled man she had envisioned, brittle as the butler. This man was in his prime, fierce and commanding, undeniably pow-erful. Too handsome by half, despite Fanny's protests. And yet, the longer she stared, the colder she grew.

Her pulse tangled between admiration and unease. Strength blazed in the set of his jaw, but his

eyes — good heavens, those eyes — were cold, calculating, almost cruel, seeming to cut into her. Power
and menace intertwined.

"Perhaps it is just as well I never met him… at
any age," she whispered more to herself than to her
companion.

Unsettled, she tore her gaze away. If this was the
measure of Collumby blood, what sort of man would
his heir prove to be? Her pulse quickened, half with
dread, half with anticipation. A man of such power
might crush her. On the other hand, he might be the
very fortress she needed against her father's tyranny.
Either way, she could not shrink from him.

A thunderclap shook the gallery.

Candle trembling in her hand, Phoebe drew her
shawl tighter with a shiver. "Come, Fanny," she murmured, though her voice had lost its earlier bravado.
"We have seen enough."

Chapter 6

The ledger blurred. Ten minutes in, and Phoebe felt she had toiled for hours.

Her gaze drifted to meet the top of his head as he hunched over the tidy list before him. She needed a conversation starter, some way to question him without being overly obvious, only nothing immediately sprang to mind. Where were her wits today?

So cheery the weather after the evening's storm, she wanted to toss the inventories into the air in a great flurry of paper and drag the man by his cravat out into the gardens to stroll the paths — and she used the word *stroll* loosely, for what she wanted was to *frolic*, but the best she could hope for from staid Mr. Ellison was a stroll. Still, better to stroll than sit. No one should stay stuffed in a study with so fine of weather to enjoy. Alas, the firm press of his lips and the notch in his brow denoted a man lost to his work, likely having forgotten her presence.

She sighed pointedly.

His quill marched across the page, steady, undisturbed, moving to the next line without the faintest hesitation.

With a huff, she turned her focus back to the list. *Why* had she volunteered for this tedium? She would learn nothing of the new earl from invoices or inventories. Mr. Ellison was purposely giving her the most innocuous tasks imaginable, clearly wise to her intentions and determined to discourage her efforts.

Silver cruets. Those were the items next on her list. She sighed again. Adjusting the sheet before her, she rewet her quill and returned to her steady scratching, copying the list of silver cruets into the ledger.

A shaft of sunlight inched across the table, teasing and tormenting her, an ever-present invitation to partake of the garden walk. She flipped to the next list. Artwork. Folding over the account's page, she began copying the items.

Drudgery.

Scratch, scratch crept her quill. Scratch, scratch echoed his. Scratch, scratch—her hand stilled. The item just scratched into the accounts was the Earl of Collumby's portrait. *The* portrait.

Airily, she said, "I saw his portrait earlier."

The quill across from her slowed.

"The late earl as St George," she continued. "A dragon at his feet. One cannot accuse him of modesty."

She eyed him to gauge his reaction.

His gaze rose to meet hers, his lips curving in the faintest of smiles. "Hardly. He was never content unless lording over something or someone."

Rather than offer embellishment, he bent his head again, back to work.

Phoebe adjusted her sheet in semblance of productivity and interest before furthering with, "Is that why he quarreled with his heir?" She spared the top of his head a brief glance.

The scrape of his nib hesitated, though this time, he kept his gaze fixed on the ledger. "Not precisely. The quarrel predates the new earl. A marriage deemed… ill-suited. To disavow the unworthy match, the branch was cut away." His tone was factual, a clerk reciting lineage, not gossip.

But Phoebe wanted more. Slipping her quill into its stand, she folded her hands before her. "Not the new earl's marriage, then?"

With a shake of his head, he said, "The new earl has yet to take a bride. The guilty party was the late earl's younger brother."

Fighting to hide her glee, she added as innocently as she could, her expression conveying only that innocent curiosity, "Our dragon slayer cut off his own brother?"

He inclined his head, but clarified, "Their father. The brother — your *almost*-betrothed — merely upheld his father's wishes once he accepted the mantle of the title."

So many more questions lingered on her lips. She had her opening to discover more. But she knew better than to press, to seem too eager for information on the earl.

"How curious," Phoebe murmured, tapping a finger against her chin. "And what of *you*, Mr. Ellison? You're well informed about family history, speaking of such things with learned ease. Not all clerks are so knowledgeable."

He looked up, meeting her squarely, their eyes locking for two long breaths before he answered. "My father taught me well to know as much about a client as possible, namely those bits they wished to remain secret. You see, Miss Whittington, my family traded indigo and cotton in Bengal. My father turned profits into shipping contracts and invested in brokerage houses in London. I grew up with ledgers thicker than sermons."

Phoebe brightened. "Ah! Then that explains how you knew of my father, the textile king."

"By name only," he replied evenly. "His ventures touch every account in the City."

Relief warmed her. So, he knew the name, but not the recent scandal. She had wondered, not particularly *worried* so much as curious. Now, if the new earl knew of the scandal or not was another matter, but about that she could concern herself with later.

She leaned forward, lashes low, voice lilting with curiosity. "But if you were brought up steeped in trade, what made you pursue law instead?"

Mr. Ellison stiffened. For the briefest moment, he faltered, as though stepping with the wrong foot or transposing numbers while reconciling an account. In a flash, he recovered. Turning back to his work, quill fresh with ink, he exuded calm as he said absently, "Numbers and law are kin enough. Both thrive on order. It seemed a… natural decision."

Phoebe bit back a triumphant smile. She had rattled him! Oh, how *delicious*.

What had upended the apple cart, she could not say, but that was unimportant. All that mattered was she *had* rattled him.

He cleared his throat, quill resuming its scratch. "Enough of me, Miss Whittington. Better you tell me—what flower suits you best? I would wager orange blossoms."

"Lilac, actually. But you may keep your guess if you like it better."

Graeme's chambers were modest by Collumby standards, well-appointed, but shorn of the ostentation that smothered the guest suites. No gilded chairs or carvings here, only a plain writing desk, a narrow hearth, and shelves already filled with orderly stacks of books and papers. Likely once the private quarters of a tutor, with its easy access to the old study. They served his purpose now, however temporary: function, not finery, a refuge from the house's grandeur he had yet to grow accustomed to.

Were such luxuries what Miss Whittington aspired to? They must be, to have accepted such an unusual arrangement with the old earl. From trade though she came, he could imagine her parading through gilt and velvet far more easily than he could imagine himself inhabiting it.

Ah, but then why had he written to his family that they would love it here? Perhaps they would. He suspected so. He wished it so.

Pulling out the desk chair, he sat heavily, rubbing the bridge of his nose. The conversation with Miss Whittington replayed itself unbidden. Her eyes teasing with mischief, her questions about trade. And then… and then *the slip*. A mere word, but enough to jolt him. Careless. He had not worn another man's name long enough for it to feel natural. Had she noticed his flinch? Yes. He had seen the spark in her eyes. What she made of it, only the Lord knew.

That was not what unsettled him most. No, it was her delight in rattling him. She had been so visibly pleased to see him falter that he almost smiled at the memory. Almost.

He tugged at his cravat. A moment to himself, to distract his thoughts from how close he had come to inviting her for a stroll in the garden, and then he would —

With a muttered oath, he shoved back the chair and retied his neckerchief. Forgetting a meeting was unlike him. That she had unsettled him enough to make him forget was the greater offense.

The corridors outside were narrow and dim, pierced only by slender, slit windows. A draft carried the scent of rain. He descended the stairs and slipped through the jib door, the heart of the house opening around him. The minstrel's hall stretched vast and echoing, its beams vaulting like the ribs of a cathedral. His stride quickened until he reached the new library.

A rap at the door. "Ellison here, when convenient."

"Come in," answered the steward.

The room smelled of leather and varnish, some shelves lined but most scarcely touched. Littering the floor, stacks of books stood like soldiers awaiting muster.

Behind a desk sat the steward, younger than Graeme expected but still wizened by age, no signs of agitation at having been kept waiting. "A matter requires your attention, sir," he said before clearing his throat. "One of the tenants in Acton Burnell has fallen six months into arrears. Ordinarily, I would appeal to the earl, but—"

"You appeal to me," Graeme finished evenly. "I speak with the earl's authority."

The man's grey head bobbed, nodding with relief. "Just so. Shall I begin proceedings for eviction?"

Letting his gaze fall to the ledger pressed towards him, Graeme studied the figures, his thumb tracing the margin. "No. Not yet. Draft a notice and add interest. If he defaults again, then we press with increasing earnest. Until then…" His attention drifted to the windowpanes, the sunny afternoon shadowed by a passing cloud—or an arriving storm. "It profits neither the earl's purse nor name to cast a family into the rain."

The steward bowed his head. "As you say, sir."

Graeme returned the ledger and turned once more to the window. Sure enough, another storm gathered on the horizon. Shame. The day had been so bright. At least Lobelia Hall was still bathed in a veil of light, the last fragments of sun before the encroaching rain.

Now, if only he could armor himself against the storm of a certain pair of bold eyes.

He pressed his palm flat on the sill, steadying himself. This was all new ground. Ledgers and contracts he knew; households, tenants, codicils, and inheritance were another world. He had already stumbled once with Miss Whittington. One slip could be excused. Another would be folly. He would learn his footing if he kept his wits. This was to be his greatest apprenticeship, after all.

Better to master his part than blunder in and lose all respect before he had earned it. He straightened, tugging his coat into place.

Tucked in Lobelia Hall's west wing was the household chapel. Candles flickered, their flames bowing from the draft that slipped around the door, casting dancing figures against the walls.

Phoebe sat midway down the pew, Fanny close to her side.

The chaplain's voice rose steady and sure: "Brethren, though the body is sown in weakness, it is raised in power. Though the grave receives us, yet in Christ we are made new creatures."

The scent of beeswax and damp stone wrinkled Phoebe's nose. She stifled a sneeze.

At the far end, Mr. Ellison occupied his own bench, posture precise as ever, prayer book balanced in his hand.

"This house, heavy with mourning, may yet rejoice, for the Lord promises that sorrow endureth but for a night, and joy cometh in the morning."

Her attention fell on the first pew. Empty. The pew where the old earl would have sat, where the new earl would soon sit, where she could sit if she won his affection. She hid a smile: the earl remained unmarried. Mr. Ellison had let slip this most important detail.

Absently, she opened the Book of Common Prayer and leafed through the pages, her fingertips brushing the frayed edges.

From across the aisle, a soft snore whistled low. When she spied the housekeeper elbowing the butler, sending his head bobbing against his chest, Phoebe smothered a smile. A glance at Mr. Ellison, however, chastised her. His head was bowed, lips moving in prayer. Chagrined to be so ill-behaved, she looked away.

The chaplain's cadence swelled like a tide. "Even as old stones may be renewed with fair mortar, so too may the heart, broken though it be, be made whole again."

Tracing the cracked spine of her book, her thoughts strayed. The chapel itself bore scars of age, colored glass long replaced with plain panes, paneling stripped to bare stone. She imagined its former beauty, mourned it, yet wondered if there was a certain grace in its renewal, readied for a new generation.

"We are not bound forever to the yoke of corruption. For Christ hath made us free, not unto license, but into righteousness."

A flicker at the high window drew her eye. A bird, wings quivering, darted into a shallow alcove where a few twig ends betrayed a hidden nest, such a fragile home, exposed and precarious… yet *free*. A cantilevered stone was all it needed. Freedom, not grandeur.

"As the bird finds its rest in the branches," the chaplain intoned, "so doth the soul find its rest in the Lord. If we walk in newness of life, then even our sorrows become but wings to lift us nearer to heaven."

Phoebe's breath caught. Could the chaplain see the bird too? No, his eyes never lifted from the page. She looked back to the alcove. The bird was gone, leaving only the faint tremor of a falling feather in its wake.

How she envied it. She had always had finery, but never freedom.

Finery had come with the price of being her father's puppet on a string, forced to dance attention on every merchant of his choosing to secure a better deal. All she had ever wanted was freedom. At one time, she had also wished for love, but she had since learned her lesson. Now, freedom alone would do.

As the chaplain's words rose and fell around her, filling her with the warmth of her heart's desire, she felt the weight of someone's gaze. Lowering her eyes from the window, she searched the pews. For some inexplicable reason, she dared another glance at Mr. Ellison, half expecting his gaze to meet hers, but although his profile was angled towards her, his eyes were trained on his book.

"See then, beloved, how one generation passeth away, and another cometh, but the earth abideth forever. Our fathers laid the foundation, we build thereupon, and they who follow shall build after us."

Phoebe's fingers tightened around her book. Had she not convinced herself only the earl could give her freedom? But if, as she had explained to Mr. Ellison, she truly sought security, not title or fortune, might there be other ways than courting an earl who was not even present?

The chaplain's voice sank into the cadence of prayer, the congregation bowing as one. "Let us, then, walk circumspectly, redeeming the time, for the days are evil. Yet even in death, the faithful are not lost, but are as seed in the ground, awaiting the Lord's harvest."

Feeling the weight, once more, of being watched, she glanced up.

This time, Mr. Ellison's gaze collided with hers.

The candlelight softened the rigid lines of his face, smoothing the scowl between his brows. For the first time, he looked… approachable.

Heat rushed to her cheeks. She dropped her lashes and fumbled to turn the page, her pulse battered too wildly to afford the words the study they demanded.

From that point forward, she heard little of the chaplain's sermon, her thoughts erratic, her awareness on a pair of kind eyes.

The service closed with the rustle of pages and the shuffle of feet on stone. Candles guttered as the small congregation of upper servants dispersed in quiet murmurs. Phoebe lingered, smoothing her gloves, unwilling to break the fragile spell of the curious and unexpected possibility that freedom might not come only by way of an earl, or more to the point, nervous her blush would betray the direction of her thoughts if she came face to face with a certain solicitor. Daylight and time would bring her back to her senses.

When at last she rose to leave, a voice spoke over her shoulder.

"Miss Whittington."

Schooling her features, Phoebe turned. Mr. Ellison stood at the end of her pew, posture as correct as ever, but his tone gentle.

"The air is clear after the storm," he said, inclining his head towards the garden. "If you would care for a walk…"

Her lips curved, a flutter of… *what*? Anticipation? Triumph?… *something wonderful* hidden in her acceptance. "Thank you, Mr. Ellison. I believe I would."

Chapter 7

A floral bouquet scented the garden, the air heady after the rain. Was it Graeme's imagination, or were the blooms brighter, as well? His vision had yet to adjust from the dimness of the chapel — yes, that must be the reason.

What had compelled him to invite Miss Whittington for a turn about the garden was a point of contention within his warring mind. He told himself it was all strategy. In a more relaxed setting, she would release her guard and may reveal intentions. The truth, however, was that he could think of little else than how determinedly his heart thumped when their eyes had met across the pews.

That her perfume mixed so intoxicatingly with the garden scents did little to dissuade his pulse, least of all when every swish of her gown accentuated the aroma.

"Does the butler always doze during the service?" she asked.

"Always." He kept his attention forward, avoiding the glimpses of her profile. "Then, I've only been in residence long enough to attend three services, including today. But during all three, the choir of snores accompanied the chaplain's sermon."

She chortled but offered no response.

They walked the length of one path in silence, he matching her strides. In his mind, he flipped through one topic after another, searching for the right anecdote, witticism, or question, but everything made him feel dull as ditch water. What does one say to a woman who is simultaneously a beautiful temptation and a suspect of fraud and greed?

Graeme slowed, gravel crunching underfoot, hands clasped loosely behind his back. "You strike me as the sort who would catalogue every flower by genus before stopping to enjoy their scent."

Miss Whittington laughed again, bright and unguarded. "So says the man brought up with ledgers as thick as sermons."

"Touché." The corner of his mouth tugged despite himself. "My mother would approve of your wit," he admitted. "She has a saying for every occasion. 'A man who steadies his voice can steady his future,' for example. That is a favorite of hers."

Miss Whittington eyed him askance, mischief glinting. "I cannot say I've known many steady men. Papa leaps from one venture to the next, thrilled by the chase. He loves nothing more than haggling, not the least interested in the outcome, only the risks and titillation of debate. Predictable in his unpredictability but hardly steady."

Graeme's curiosity sharpened. If her father was so wealthy, why this desperate scheme? He pressed no further, though, and silence lapsed until she filled it.

"You mentioned your mother. Do you see her often?"

"Until recently, I lived with her and my sister. Both are in London still." Fondness warmed his tone.

"Are you eager to return to them?"

"Yes and no. My plan is to take up residence at Lobelia Hall. I confess I had been unsure if this would be the case, as I had wished to see the state of the hall first, namely, after the rumors of the unpleasantness of the late earl. I did not know if I would find a hall in disrepair, angry tenants, disloyal staff, or other surprises. I can now say I'm pleased with all before me and hope my family will join soon." After a moment's deliberation, he added, "The earl will need me."

Her smile teased. "And your wife? Will she be joining, as well?"

His pulse quickened.

"No." The single word was quiet, decisive. Then, lest she misunderstand, he iterated, "No wife."

The silence this time was easier, companionable. Miss Whittington paused before a stone cherub nestled in an alcove and considered it for some time.

Clearing his throat, he asked, "Could you have been happy here?"

Rather than look at him, her gaze lifted to the pigeonholes in the stone. She took her time in answering, so long that he wondered if she would ignore the question. At length she asked, "Did you see the chapel window?"

He looked at the stonework, curious how that reminded her of the chapel window.

"There's a bird nesting in the alcove. I couldn't stop watching it during the service."

Graeme angled a glance at her. "A bird?"

"Yes." She laughed lightly, but then her words tumbled out, unguarded. "It struck me how free it seemed. No ledgers to balance, no bargains to strike, no marriages to arrange. Just a perch, a patch of sky, and the will to fly." She pressed her lips together, her cheeks flushed. "Silly, I suppose."

"Not silly," he said, softer than he intended.

Her animation surprised him, the brightness in her eyes so different from the careful poise she usually wore. For a fleeting moment, he saw not a schemer to be questioned or a guest to be managed, but simply a woman with her heart laid bare.

"That doesn't answer your question, does it?" she asked, ambling away from the statue, her steps light, careless. "It's not a place or a person for which I pine, not title or fortune, only the freedom to make my own choices. I can be happy anywhere if I had that." She laughed, heartily at first, but then with an edge of cynicism. "I suddenly realized I have more in common with the new earl than I thought possible. We're both bound by the circumstances of our birth, he to his title and I to my father. Neither of us has much choice in life, do we?"

Graeme saw a great deal of difference in their circumstances, but rather than voice that, his thoughts strayed unwittingly to the codicil. "Would wealth not buy you freedom?"

"As in a dowry?" she said crisply. "They purchase husbands, not freedom."

Her words landed between them like a rook blocking his path. He slowed, searching for a reply that would not sound like a rebuke or a lie. None came.

By the time they reached the end of the path, she had recovered her composure, smiling as if nothing had been said. Yet he could feel the board reset beneath them, pieces shifting for the next play.

Chapter 8

Two days later, she wandered the garden alone. Her thoughts, however, insisted she keep company with a certain solicitor.

Despite the heavy clouds pressing low after a morning of sunshine, she could not resist the call of the blooms, sweeter than any London park she had known. The air was lush with damp earth and roses.

If she had her own home, she would want a garden just like this.

Phoebe seated herself on a stone bench opposite the cherub, palms resting on the cool surface. Something had shifted on Sunday. She could not pinpoint *what*, only that Mr. Ellison no longer appeared merely a stiff clerk. His nearness had made her breath falter. Ridiculous, really. Their talks had only ever been about accounts and lineage, hardly fodder for romance. And yet, she could not deny her *awareness* of him.

A sudden rustle cut short her thoughts. From around the hedge, a floppy-eared dog skittered, tongue lolling, paws skidding on the gravel to come nose-to-skirt with her. Phoebe reached down to pet her new companion only to be startled yet again when a small boy bounded after it, arms outstretched, laughter squealing.

"Steady there!" she called, rising as the dog circled her skirts.

His cheeks pink from the chase, the child clutched the dog's scruff. "Caught him at last! He never listens, miss!"

"Then you are both conqueror and puppy keeper." Phoebe smiled in reward.

The boy returned a proud grin, holding fast to the dog. But before she could ask his name, two older children hurried into view, halting short when they saw her.

A girl, perhaps twelve, but as solemn as a little matron, gathered her skirts and dropped into a hasty curtsy. "We've not had the pleasure of an introduction, miss."

Phoebe inclined her head. "No, though your brother has already claimed me as his new friend. What am I to do but submit?"

Before the older brother could say his piece, voices rose in conversation behind them as another pair turned the hedge. This was becoming a popular alcove, Phoebe mused. Their parents appeared at the turn of the path, surprise flickering sharply in their faces. She could almost hear their unasked question: *Who was this woman, alone in the earl's garden, without a proper host or chaperone, and with their children no less?* Quite beyond the pale.

The younger boy was still clutching the dog and chattering happily, unaware of the impending trouble of both chasing a dog and talking with a stranger.

Phoebe rose to the occasion with graceful composure, her curtsy unhurried. "It seems I am discovered, though not by design, I assure you. Your young explorer found me out. He has proved quite the gallant guide, though I daresay he needs no help from me in finding mischief."

The child puffed with pride, although Phoebe could not say if it were from being heralded a gallant guide or a finder of mischief.

Phoebe added warmly, "I am but a guest of the house, taking advantage of the sunshine between rain showers. Your son's company has been the happiest accident of my stay."

It was the father who spoke first, genially, his chuckle proving Phoebe had won herself a new ally. "Not every day Rutherford is called a happy accident."

The mother, however, stood to her full height — barely reaching Phoebe's shoulder — and said in crisp tones, "We've been paying our respects to Mrs. Redshaw. We presume you are kin to his lordship?"

Although Phoebe's lips parted, it was a deep and steady voice from behind her that answered. "Miss Whittington is here under the earl's invitation." Mr. Ellison stepped forward, ruffling the dog's ears. "I serve as his man of business. We thank you for your condolences and trust we may return your card shortly."

With murmured farewells, the family withdrew, the children waving as they were shepherded away.

Phoebe turned, lashes lowered in mock coyness. "How delightful to have you come to my rescue."

"On the contrary. I was rescuing the household's reputation." The gleam in his eyes betrayed his humor.

"Then it was *I* who rescued *you* with my quick wit, smoothing matters before you arrived."

Blue eyes twinkled. "I see you require no knight to defend you."

"No indeed." She pivoted to admire the flowerbed, only to glance back over her shoulder when she said, "Though I confess, it gratifies me to know you were ready to brandish a lance, on behalf of the household or otherwise."

He matched her smile with dry wit. "Perhaps you should attempt another scandal, if only to test my readiness."

"Don't tempt me," she quipped.

"For someone with no claim to the stage, you play the lady of the house convincingly."

Her hand pressed to her heart. "Take care, sir. A reproach disguised as a compliment might lead me to believe you're sincere."

He laughed outright, the sound caught between admiration and caution, and for an instant neither broke the gaze that lingered too long.

With a glance towards the house, he asked, "Join me in the old study tomorrow? We've more work to catalogue."

Dipping into a teasing curtsy, Phoebe said, "Then I shall come prepared for the task."

Graeme slid a long roll of parchment across the desk, the edges curling like stubborn ivy. "Tenant rolls," he explained, smoothing the creases flat. "Names, holdings, rents due. The steward's writing, however, leaves much to be desired."

Miss Whittington cocked her head. "And why have they been given to you? I shouldn't think a solicitor cares much for tenant rolls."

Astute woman, he thought. Aloud, he said, "The earl wishes a full accounting, from tenants to tassels. We must copy the notes in a neat hand and order them properly."

"Doesn't he trust the steward?" Miss Whittington nosed.

"A man of business neither trusts nor distrusts without cause. More to the point, the earl insists on knowing what he has inherited, and so we must catalogue until our eyes cross."

"Then I fear my eyes have already failed me." She squinted at the parchment.

Graeme leaned to read the crabbed script, but the words blurred without his spectacles.

"This says," she continued with exaggerated solemnity, "Widow Parsons pays her rent in… *chickens*."

Tugging the roll closer, convinced she jested, he secured his spectacles. Sure enough. Four lines from the top: *chickens*.

His lips twitched.

"How many hens equal a pound, do you suppose?" she asked.

"Three," he replied without inflection. "Provided they lay golden eggs. Otherwise, she's in arrears."

Miss Whittington stared for three full breaths, then burst into laughter — unguarded, musical, and altogether charming. Graeme's pulse leapt.

"And I always thought ledgers were dull," she said, dabbing at her eyes. "Never did I dream poultry would feature. Do you always accept hens in payment, Mr. Ellison?"

"Only when their solicitors are in attendance," he returned, the corner of his mouth betraying him.

She laughed again, shaking her head. "I daresay the poor woman has probably paid thus for years. Surely the earl won't object?"

"Unlikely," he admitted. "Still, Mrs. Parsons may merit a visit from a curious clerk. After all, I wouldn't wish to... run afoul with the tenants."

"Run *a fowl*?" Miss Whittington's laughter pealed. "For such a *poultry* amount! But don't forget to collect the hens while you're there."

Graeme tried to stifle his smile but could no longer smother it from view. "Perhaps you'll accompany me. You seem the sharper negotiator."

Her brows arched. "Me? Whatever could you mean?"

His glance flicked briefly to her maid, absorbed in her knitting. "Mrs. Redshaw goes into Tansy Hollow soon, errands for the household. I've been pressed to accompany her. You might take the chance to see the village?"

"Oh!" Surprise lit her face. "Oh, I should be delighted."

For once, he resisted another jest, unwilling to mar the glow of her acceptance. Instead, he turned back to the parchment, though his quill lay idly above the page. Each glimpse of her smile from the corner of his eye was too arresting. Likewise, the faint scratch of her notetaking, the soft clink of needles in the corner, and the scent of neroli perfume seemed suddenly too loud, too close, too aromatic.

Her voice startled him from his reverie. "You've spoken of your mother and sister. Do they never fear losing you to the endless paperwork with your change of occupation from tradesman to solicitor?"

"On the contrary. They would lock me in the study if they were here, ensure I stayed focused and served the earldom to the best of my abilities. My sister claims it's the only way to keep me out of trouble."

"Mmm. She sounds wise."

"She is thirteen."

"Ah." Miss Whittington laughed again, warm and unrestrained. "I hope she'll like Lobelia Hall. But will Mrs. Ellison not miss London?"

His mind stuttered. "Who?"

She blinked. "Mrs. Ellison. Your mother?"

Recovering, he bent low over the parchment as if it held all his interest. "Ah, yes, of course. I mean, no, I think not. She and my sister are avid readers. Between the two libraries here, I doubt London will be missed."

Miss Whittington studied him for a moment, her curiosity obviously piqued. Graeme forced his attention back to the page, pulse thudding in his ears. A narrow escape.

After a moment, he tapped the parchment with the end of his quill. "See? Books upon books. Enough to occupy them for years and distract them from any missed London diversions. Much like you — too occupied teasing me about hens to notice time passing."

"Then I fear you are doomed, sir, for I shall not soon forget Widow Parsons."

Their eyes met across the desk, his guarded, hers still bright with laughter. The air between them held both warmth and question, their gazes lingering longer than propriety allowed.

With smooth, steady strokes, Fanny brushed Phoebe's hair, the curls unfurling against her shoulders.

Phoebe studied her reflection, though her thoughts wandered. What would the Phoebe of old think now? That girl would be aghast. Waiting in a stranger's house for the chance to ensnare an earl? This was just the sort of game her father would approve, the very sort the old Phoebe would have rebelled against, for *that* Phoebe believed in hearts above all things, without question or caution. But hearts, once bruised, were treacherous companions. One did not recover quickly from being duped into an elopement, least of all with a libertine's honeyed vows of love — false vows. She would not be fooled again. She would not be played for money. She would not —

A sigh escaped as the bristles soothed her scalp.

And yet... how many "would nots" did it take to muffle the beat of a heart? Something *had* shifted in the chapel, something she could not undo. She could no longer see Mr. Ellison as a staid clerk, but rather as an attractive and available man. To call it infatuation would be absurd. One walk, a few shared laughs — hardly the stuff of love. But the shortness of her breath? Undeniable.

Perhaps it was only that he was nothing like Freddy. But even that comparison was unjust. Mr. Ellison was not a measure against her past.

The mirror offered no answers, only her own searching gaze. And so, the trouble remained: aside from her cautions and her bruised pride, what reason had she *not* to care for him? The earl himself meant nothing, only a means to freedom from her father's hold. More to the point, the earl was not here, and Mr. Ellison was, but more profoundly, she felt an attraction for the clerk, a connection, beyond their shared experiences in trade, something more acute, something that trembled her knees.

Could she risk her heart again? There was more at stake than her heart, though, and she would do well to remember that fact.

Freedom. Always freedom. His question echoed: *Would wealth buy you freedom?* If she had money of her own, perhaps. But young ladies did *not* live alone in cottages without scandal. Should she purchase a little place of her own, her life would be as steeped in scandal as the one she had left in London. Even liberty came with shackles.

Her reflection in the mirror seemed to smirk back. It asked, demanded even: *Which chain will you bear?* The risk of love, the wager of an absent earl, or the prison of her father's demands?

For now, she let the worry rest. In time, she hoped her heart would tell her which dreams to keep and which to let go.

Chapter 9

The estate cart, a sturdy single-horse convey-
ance with no pretensions, jolted as it left
the Hall's smooth gravel for the rutted lane
winding into Tansy Hollow. Phoebe steadied herself against the squabs, her shawl wrapped about her
shoulders. At least today, she was properly attired in
a dyed gown rather than relying solely on the black
silk to express mourning.

The housekeeper had protested using the carriage
when they first set out, but Mr. Ellison managed to
convince her — after all, he had posed, this would
encourage procuring more provisions than she would
have otherwise. Mumbling that she would not mind
a stop at the apothecary and bakery, and, oh, perhaps
the haberdashery, as well, she agreed that having the
carriage was the sensible choice.

Phoebe glanced out at the scatter of cottages
beyond the trees, smoke curling cheerily from their
chimneys.

Mrs. Redshaw, sitting opposite, gestured towards
the hedgerows. "This way has seen generations of feet.
All manner of carts and carriages, and still it holds
firm. Masters come and go, but the Hollow remains."

Phoebe tilted her head in amusement. "You make it sound indestructible."

"And near enough it is, miss. Long after we are dust, the tenants will till the same soil, the bells will toll at the same church. That is the comfort of a village. Continuity."

Continuity. How unlike her own life, tossed on her father's whims.

Beside her, a low voice cut into her thoughts. "Continuity may be a comfort," Mr. Ellison murmured, gaze on the road, "but it is also expectation. Every man knows the eyes of his neighbors are upon him, weighing if he holds steady or falters."

Mrs. Redshaw hummed in satisfaction, as though he had proved her point.

Phoebe, however, turned his words over. A village might be charming, yes, but it could also be a cage. At least for some. Although she did not think it was to the village he referred, but to what, then? The new earl's position? His own position as solicitor?

The lane dipped, and suddenly the Hollow opened before them: stone cottages, a baker's boy darting across with steaming loaves, geese scattering. Phoebe leaned forward, lips parting. Smaller than London, yes, but so *alive*. How quickly she had dismissed it when she first passed through.

The cart rocked to a stop with the creaking groan of harness and leather. The party spilled out, Mrs. Redshaw brisk with purpose, two maids trailing. Phoebe breathed deeply. The air was thick with scents: peat smoke, lavender bundles, warm bread, the faint sourness of wet wool drying in the sun.

Children darted past, chasing the geese, laughter filling the air. Voices rose all around them, sellers calling, dogs barking, hens cackling. How had she been so mistaken during her first impression? The village was quaint, but lively and charming. Oh, what an injustice she had done it before! At the time, she had only recognized its size, and pointedly, how it was not London. But now, that *was* the point. It was *not* London. Tansy Hollow was full of *life*! All so unlike London's busy anonymity, all greed and speed. *This* was altogether different. *This* was genuine and unhurried. Her heart yearned.

The damp grit of gravel crunched underfoot, interspersed with the squelch of mud. Passersby lifted their hems, picking their way around the puddles from last night's rain, their half-boots already muddy.

Mrs. Redshaw guided them past a shop decorated with woven baskets overflowing with turnips, carrots with fronds still attached, and bunches of herbs tied with twine. The sharp tang of vinegar from pickled vegetables in jars had Phoebe wrinkling her nose. Nearly everyone they passed paid Mrs. Redshaw a deferential nod, sparing Phoebe and Mr. Ellison curious glances. Phoebe shrugged off their side-eye looks.

As Mrs. Redshaw stopped to haggle with the apothecary, the maids wandered off. Phoebe and Mr. Ellison lingered at the street's edge. She drank in the surroundings.

At her side, Mr. Ellison leaned close, voice low. "I've my eye on a sweet roll once we're finished here."

She blinked, surprised by the mischief in his tone. "So, you *can* be tempted."

His mouth quirked. "Even clerks must eat."

"You mentioned your mother has a saying for every circumstance," she teased. "What would she say now? Perhaps, 'A man who covets sweet rolls cannot covet scandal'?"

His sidelong look made her laugh before he spoke. "She would say worse, I promise you, but that is quite close."

As they wandered, Phoebe plucked a lavender sprig from one of the bundles hanging at a shop front. "I should very much like to meet her. Do you think she'll like Tansy Hollow?"

"She will," he said softly. "She's long wanted the countryside. It'll be a welcome change to Reading."

Her twirling of the lavender slowed. "I thought you said she lives in London."

"Nearly. The family business is in London. My mother sees little difference between the two. Now, I can give her the quiet life she desires."

"How enviable," Phoebe murmured absently, tucking the sprig into the folds of her shawl. "To have both quiet and a place to belong. I can't think your sister would like it as much, being so young—do not all young girls wish for the clamor of Town?"

"She'll make herself an authority on village life within her first week here." His mouth curved faintly. "She fancies herself an authority on everything, you must know."

Phoebe laughed. "And an authority on tedious brothers?"

"The two of you would be fast friends."

Their eyes met, the moment stretching. He smiled first, his blue eyes bright with amusement.

"May I be so bold as to ask her name?"

"Harriet." Attention fixed on Phoebe, he followed with, "And you? Any siblings?"

"Not a one. I'm the apple of my father's eye."

"And so doted on, you're now rotten to the core, I presume."

She grinned. "You presume correctly, but then, everyone loves a bit of devilry."

They walked past two more terraced shops and a half dozen more curious looks from villagers before Phoebe spoke again, feeling altogether bold to know her companion better, mostly, she reasoned, because the silly man could not stop stealing glances at her.

"What will become of your family's trade business now that you've taken a different route?" She eyed him askance to steal glimpses of her own. Was it her imagination, or did the sunlight burnish his dusty brown hair gold?

He cleared his throat, the smile that had been playing at the corners of his lips dipping. "To be honest, Miss Whittington, this has been on my mind a great deal lately. The business is my grandfather's legacy, passed now through two generations. I—" he paused both his progress and his words, clasping his hands behind him. Meeting her gaze, he finished, "I believe the business has served its purpose. I can now grant my family their long-held wish of moving away from the city. It is my opinion that my grandfather and father, both, would approve of the decision."

Phoebe studied him, surprised by his candor. The man she met in the study was a different man than the one standing before her. Oh, they were both Mr. Ellison, of course, but the man in the study was... well... *clerical*. This man stood tall and proud, a man in control of family and fate. He was a far cry from the powerful and oppressive gentleman she had seen in the Earl of Collumby's portrait, but she could not deny the commanding poise Mr. Ellison exuded, however much unaware of it he likely was. His steady gaze gave her an unexpected thrill. Would he shrink back into his tidy role when they next met in the study, or would she recognize this new version of him?

He guided them forward before asking, "Do you believe in pre-ordained destiny?"

"Are we to digress into theological conversation now? Talk of the weather would be far superior if you're in want of a topic."

With a chuckle, he said, "Another time, then, perhaps. I daresay you've tricked me with your intimate questions into spilling my musings, Miss Nose."

Rather than elicit a response, he invited her to step into the draper's shop. His distraction worked, for her eyes widened as the bright colors of ribbons and silks drew her under their spell. Her fingertips brushed a bolt of lilac satin before reaching for the ribbons. Not entirely appropriate for mourning, but...

"How is it, Mr. Ellison, that even in a village no larger than a thimble, I find temptations enough to empty a purse?"

In hushed tones, Mr. Ellison said, "Shopkeepers have a keen eye for weakness. Yours, apparently, is lilac."

Glancing sharply, she said, "You presume much from one ribbon."

"You've touched it twice."

She arched a brow. "Insufferable spy."

"Only methodical," he countered. "I notice patterns. First, your confession for lilac scent and now…" He nodded to the ribbons.

"And now I am a *pattern* to be studied?" Their eyes held a moment too long before she laughed, turning back to the ribbons. "If you are quite finished cataloguing me, sir, you may return to your poultry accounts. Hens are easier company, I'm certain."

With a hearty chuckle, he leaned closer, his shoulder brushing hers, just as Mrs. Redshaw reappeared, her arms laden with parcels.

"The village watches for the new earl," the housekeeper announced in way of greeting. "I'll rest easier when he's here at last, then I can stop fielding questions I don't know how to answer. Tell me, when is he due?"

Mr. Ellison stiffened almost imperceptibly, but his tone remained even. "Soon enough. Until then, Lobelia Hall is well managed."

Phoebe caught the faint tension under his calm but smoothed it with a smile of her own. "In the meantime, we mustn't keep ourselves from that promised sweet roll."

Curiously, now, the earl's arrival was an event she would rather delay. Her place as a guest was precarious enough, as she was only invited in anticipation of the earl. Once he arrived, she would have overstayed her welcome.

Sometime later, Phoebe settled into the carriage seat, a few parcels at her feet, one including lilac ribbons. The sway was oddly soothing as the bustle of Tansy Hollow receded down quiet lanes. She risked a glance at Mr. Ellison only to catch his gaze on her.

Warmth curled in her chest. Their knees brushed —
briefly, all to do with the rocking of the carriage — the
touch catching Phoebe's breath. Politely, he shifted
aside, but his half-smile betrayed him. She turned to
the scenery, her skin tingling where her dress had
met his breeches.

The ghost of his smile lingered with her all the
way to Lobelia Hall.

Chapter 10

Untangling the length of twine binding a stack of estate correspondences, Graeme lifted his eyes to the clock... again. Five minutes late. A wiser man would take this as a sign to return to reason, to stay at the desk and finish the tenant accounts, to play the solicitor and nothing more.

But he was not feeling particularly wise.

In fact, he was feeling—

The door opened.

Miss Whittington swept inside with a breeze of orange blossoms, a hopeful smile, and her usual poise. "What enterprise today, Mr. Ellison? Have you a list of broken teacups requiring inventory?"

"Only if you insist on documenting each chip and crack yourself," he said, masking his grin by pretending to straighten the parchments before him. "Though I confess I've lost heart for indoor tasks."

She lifted a brow. "An ailment I had not thought capable of afflicting you."

"The sun is wickedly persuasive," he said with a peek at the nearest window. "Shall we risk Mrs. Redshaw's ire? We will take the work to the garden and claim virtue for having read estate accounts in fresh air."

Miss Whittington gave a sham sigh of defeat. "I should not like to be held responsible for a clerk led astray by good weather."

"You mistake me for a disciplined man."

Her responding laugh tugged something tight and pleasing inside him. "Is this rebellion?" she teased. "I should have thought you too steady for such impulses."

She would not have used the word *steady* if she could hear his heartbeat.

Notably leaving both ledgers and correspondences on the desk, he offered his arm. When she took it — so easily, without hesitation or question — his pulse stuttered. He had offered her an escort before. But this, for a brief moment, felt different. Felt... natural, and altogether dangerous.

They left the maid behind in the study and stepped into the warm hush of early afternoon. Bees buzzed low over the hedges, the gravel path gleaming pale under the sun.

Miss Whittington inhaled deeply, then let a contented sigh escape. "One can almost forget what strain of duty presses indoors."

"That is precisely my intention."

Their steps slowed where the path narrowed, lined by parterres and a trickle of water from a garden fountain.

"Tell me, Mr. Ellison," she began, eyes not on him but forward, as though the air itself had pried loose a lingering question. "How did you come into the Earl of Collumby's service? Or did you always intend to be a solicitor to a peer once you traded indigo for law?"

Graeme kept his gaze ahead lest he betray the truth on his face. "We crossed paths in London. The earl never expected to inherit, and so once the estate solicitor found him and broke the news, that once humble gentleman desired a man of law, his own, not one tied to the estate. The cordial Mr. Ellison won his favor for the task, having offered legal advice previously."

That, at least, was true. He spoke easier when he could share truths, even if she would understand the meaning differently.

Her lips curved. "A ringing endorsement of your talents."

"It suited us both, he needing unbiased perspective on inheritance matters and the learned Mr. Ellison wanting the challenge."

"And so, you walked away from your father's business," she said softly, as though filing the fact with respectful curiosity. "How noble. Did the earl approve of such independence?"

"As it happened, the learned gentleman in question required no endorsement from anyone on the matter." Another half-truth, but spoken with just as much wryness as remembrance.

"How long have you known him, only since the inheritance?"

"Err... longer." He racked his memory, searching for another grain of truth, namely when one Mr. Lockwood of the severed line had met one Mr. Ellison, Esq. "Perhaps five years."

She hummed, stealing a glance up at him beneath tremulous eyelashes. "He must have been persuasive to acquire you. Tell me you did not find a bee in your bonnet and suddenly decide to cast in with aristocrats."

"Not a bee," he said cautiously. "Something more like... disquiet."

She looked at him fully, then, eyes wide and unguarded. "I understand disquiet very well."

And he believed her. Perhaps more deeply than she suspected.

That she fell into her own thoughts rather than question his meaning was a relief, for he did not know how to answer without exposing more of his life than he ought.

They passed beneath a rose arch where he paused at the fork in the path. The sunlight fell warm across her hair, coaxing mahogany depths from her dark curls.

"And what of you and the late earl?" he asked. "You had said your father exchanged letters with him this summer. Did you, as well?"

"No," she answered without hesitation. "The man was a stranger to me. All of this is still rather... strange to me." She gestured around the grand garden, then let her hand fall, as though the moment had revealed something vulnerable she had not intended.

He let that sit for a beat, then, gently, said, "And yet, here you are."

"Yes, and here I am." Her smile tipped, wry and a little sad. "For that matter, here *you* are, Mr. Ellison. We are both in places we were never meant to be."

Something pricked at him. Not pity so much as kinship. As if a string had been tied between them in that small remark, drawn taut by shared displacement.

"Tell me," he said as he steered them down the shaded walk where the cherub stood sentinel, its marble face angled skyward. "If you had your choice of destination, where *would* you be?"

"Anywhere without a ledger!" She laughed gaily at first, but then, after seeing something in his face he could not himself see, she added with a somber brow, "Anywhere a man cannot take it upon himself to decide my worth."

His breath stilled. Her words, however lightheartedly said, held honesty. He also heard the bruised thread beneath them.

Swallowing, he braved, "Would you hold it against me if I said you are decidedly worth knowing?"

Her stride faltered.

He steadied her with a hand cradled beneath her elbow.

She said nothing at first, only tugged at a curl and looked from the cherub to the distant treetops, as though the world had become too fragile to stand still beneath.

Before he could apologize for the remark or claim it a jest, she tipped her head towards him with a returning spark. "And what of you, Mr. Ellison? Have you ever met an earl before all this?"

Graeme's mouth tugged in rueful amusement. "Only one. I... endured the encounter."

"You'll forgive me, but the way you carry yourself, I had assumed attendance amongst nobles."

"I assure you, if I appear polished, it is merely the reflection of my spectacles."

Her laugh, this time, was full of music and bright with surprise. Something inside him yielded. He reached out without thinking and tucked the curl behind her ear. The contact was brief, but his thumb brushed her cheek. The warmth lingered.

"Now your turn, Miss Whittington. Have *you* ever met an earl?"

"Yes and no," she said with a self-conscious titter. "I've been introduced to several noblemen at soirees, but no one I could later meet in a crowd and claim familiarity. No one, that is, except a marchioness and, through her, the marquess, but the acquaintance is one of circumstance rather than intimacy. That is the extent of my illustrious friendships. You see, nothing so grand compared to your position as the great advisor to an earl."

He chuckled. "Not so great, only a modest man treading in boots too large for him."

"You are *not* the humble clerk you claim to be," she said, low and direct. "You speak as if you were born to command. I see it every time you step forward. There is nothing of the timid about you."

His chest tightened. "And yet my training is… insufficient for what's required."

"No man needs training to prove good character. A pox on titles and fortunes. Courage is what gives a man stature, and I see before me a brave man stepping into daunting responsibility."

He stopped.

So did she.

Sunlight filtered through a passing cloud. Her gaze was bold and unrelenting; her chin lifted just enough to keep her dignity and her soft uncertainty in the same glance.

He swallowed. Could not speak. Words, suddenly, were a poor vessel for what hung between them.

Then—

"Mr. Ellison, sir. A letter!"

They both turned as the butler shuffled down the path towards them, a sealed missive held aloft.

Miss Whittington stepped away quickly, her composure as swift and graceful as the flutter of a bird's wings settling into stillness. The spell was broken… just slightly, just long enough to remind him of *danger*. Of timing. Of everything he had not yet said.

While her attention was on the butler, Graeme stole one last, lingering glance, unable to stop the flicker of regret.

She saw it.

Her eyes sought his, stealing a glance of her own, and he knew the moment she caught his bold expression of longing. But she smiled, just enough to promise nothing had truly been lost. At least, not yet.

The letter blurred.

Graeme dragged a hand across his face and forced himself to read it for the fifth time, as if repetition might turn sense into madness, or the reverse. Thank the Lord he had torn the seal and read the letter alone.

The estate solicitor's response to his initial inquiry was thorough. Too thorough. The facts — if they were facts — were plain enough:

One year prior, the late Earl of Collumby had issued a formal offer of marriage to Miss Phoebe Whittington. She had declined. Instead, she had accepted a proposal from the impoverished Marquess of Pickering and, according to the solicitor, was even now living in Yorkshire as the Marchioness.

Which made the woman upstairs a liar.

A fraud.

And he, Graeme, a fool.

He shoved back from the desk, reaching for fresh parchment with numb fingers, anger guiding his quill rather than sense. Before long, a hasty letter to the Marquess of Pickering had been sealed — by the Collumby crest of all things — and given to the butler for posting. It was not until the study door closed behind Mr. Willet that the enormity of the blunder struck him.

The letter should have gone from solicitor to solicitor. Ellison to Barmby. Not earl to marquess. And certainly not with such graceless haste.

He sank into his chair, elbows on the desk, head in his hands.

Was this how easily he could be undone? A single letter. And he trusted a stranger's word over the woman who had just an hour ago confessed knowing a marquess and marchioness? She had been honest. Or close enough. Why, then, had he been so ready to doubt her?

He wanted, desperately, to send for her now, demand truth, explanation, anything to ease the sting of betrayal. But no. That was not justice. That was vanity, seeking proof he had not been taken in by a pretty face and a handful of clever smiles.

He breathed out, shaken.

There had to be another way. But it required something he was no longer sure he possessed.

Trust.

And the question that knotted his insides was not whether Phoebe Whittington was lying. It was whether he had ever given her the chance to tell the truth.

Chapter 11

Balancing the tray on one hip, Phoebe rapped on the study door.

"Come," came the muffled response from within.

On a deep breath, she entered, the door creaking.

Late afternoon sunlight glazed the tall windows, casting long shadows across the room and gilding piles of papers, scattered books, and a creased letter she recognized as the one Mr. Willet had delivered earlier. A candle stub, half melted, leaned precariously towards the desk's disarray.

Mr. Ellison looked up with surprise. His gaze flicked to the closed door behind her, likely noting the absence of her maid, then to the tea tray, then finally to her.

"I bring an end to your dreadful solitude," she said, setting the tray down and brandishing the small leather journal she had tucked beneath her arm. "And tea. Mostly tea." With a blush, she added, "You may consider this bribery to spare us tomorrow's session of ledger-induced ennui, for once you see what I've found, you'll surely wish to devote our morning to examining it further."

She expected a wry quip in response, perhaps even a smile. Instead, he simply rose and bowed, slow and polite.

"You look as though Mr. Willet delivered a thundercloud. Have I come at an inopportune time?"

For a moment, his expression opened with a flash of something weary, unsettled. But it shuttered again, as he gestured for her to sit with a civil, practiced smile that did not reach his eyes.

"Just one of life's little surprises," he said.

Phoebe sat, heart ticking faster than she would like to admit. After the walk in the gardens... after his warm regard and gentle touch... this chill in him felt wrong. She glanced askance at the letter on the desk...

Pouring tea into his cup, she held her silence. Across from her, Mr. Ellison watched. After all her fretting over the breach in decorum, of him thinking her too forward, *this* was his reaction to her surprise visit. Had she misread him, and thus miscalculated her decision?

"I've been thinking, Miss Whittington, about something you said earlier." He paused to clear his throat of its scratchiness. "How *well* do you know the Marquess of Pickering and his wife?"

Her hand froze, the teapot mid-tilt over her cup.

She had *not* given him the name of the marquess and marchioness of her acquaintance. Her memory would not fail her on this point.

She eyed the desk again, her gaze catching the folded edge of the letter's parchment. Ah. Yes, well, it had only been a matter of time before he heard of the scandal. Inevitable, really. Had the new earl written to him, then? Or someone else? How much of the scandal he knew was the more important question.

She set the teapot down carefully. "Should I assume this inquiry is connected to whatever it is Mr. Willet delivered?"

He said nothing, neither in denial nor admittance.

She angled her chin. "I'd wager that crumpled letter holds at least one version of my life. Might I know which one it is?"

His eyes widened. Mr. Ellison leaned back as though she had knocked the breath from him. Then, haltingly, he exhaled and cleared his throat. "That is... bold of you, Miss Whittington."

"A specialty of mine, I assure you. You're welcome to read the letter aloud, if you prefer. I would rather we not pretend a casual conversation between acquaintances if there are accusations to which I must apply. Have out with it."

Rather than reply, he studied her, but then, to her astonishment, he rose to retrieve the letter before handing it to her.

She unfolded it with steady fingers, every instinct coiled against the expected blow. The more she read, however, the words revealing nothing more scandalous than proposals made, declined, and redirected, the more an incredulous laugh bubbled up in her chest, until a soft laugh escaped her parted lips.

"*This* is the source of your brooding?" she asked, both amused and relieved as she handed the letter back. "A rumor of a wedding that never was?"

"You did decline a proposal," he pointed out.

"And accepted another," she agreed with a nod. "I imagine half the eligible ladies in London could be convicted of the same crime."

Although he watched her closely, there was no hardness in his eyes, only something almost sheepish.

"In my defense," he said, rubbing the back of his neck, "the wording suggests you are already a marchioness."

"Ah. But sadly, no. I would make a terrible marchioness. Everyone knows they are required to look regal in velvet at *least* once a week. A burden too great, even for me."

"I confess, I believed the worst. That is, if Miss Whittington were in Yorkshire now, then…"

"Thank you for the admission." She settled comfortably with her teacup, taking her time with a sip. "Last year, my father offered a handsome dowry to see me settled, to his advantage, of course. The two proposals he favored were from the Earl of Collumby and the Marquess of Pickering, as you've surmised. I declined the earl in favor of the marquess… but it was not what I wanted, not truly. In the end, the marquess married someone else, someone *not* named Phoebe Whittington, I might add. His wife and I remain friends, of a sort."

Maintaining composure, she looked past him at the fading light; the garden basked in a golden glow. No reason to mention Freddy. Yet. No reason to mention *who* the marquess married. Yet. She drank her tea in silence.

At length, she clarified, "I am not hiding a secret marriage in Yorkshire, Mr. Ellison, nor am I someone other than who I claim to be."

She set her saucer on the tray, wondering whether to take the journal and leave. While nothing about the scandal had been said, at least not yet, she had lost the spark that had driven her to share the mischievous treasure. Now all she wanted was the privacy of the bedchamber.

Phoebe watched him, trying to read his expression.

He sat back, tea cooling in his hands, his gaze fixed on her in return, only it was not sharp with accusation as she had feared, rather thoughtful, almost soft. When he spoke, his voice was quiet but meaningful. "I'm a fool to have thought otherwise, even for a second."

A simple admission. But something in the way he said it, and that he said it, loosened the knot that had tightened beneath her ribs.

With deliberate calm, he set down his teacup. "I appreciate your honesty, Miss Whittington. I deserve to be chided for believing such an outlandish claim. Curiosity was poor practice on my part. You'll be calling *me* Mr. Nose now." A faint, smile ghosted across his lips, one that spoke to her of self-mockery. "I should have trusted what I already knew: that you've never been anything less than forthright with me."

Phoebe blinked. Warmth crept up the back of her neck. "I... I... thank you," she managed. Relief, surprising in its intensity, softened her shoulders. "Thank you for saying so, Mr. Nose."

A huff of genuine amusement escaped him.

The air between them eased, not back to the intimacy shared in the garden, but no longer sharp-edged. She smiled the kind of smile that bridged silences.

He nodded towards the journal. "And this… this is the reason I'm to be bribed out of tomorrow's ledgers?"

She nudged the volume closer. "Of *this*, I am entirely guilty. I found it, nestled between enough dust to bury a regiment, while *nosing* about upstairs. I couldn't resist. Can you guess what it is?" Before he could reply, she answered, "The late earl's personal journal. It turns out the late earl had a habit of writing meticulous notes of all manner of opinions, blunt ones at that, about everyone from tenants to parsons. He rarely bothered with names, however, offering us decoding-over-tea mysteries to solve. Does this opening entry entice you? 'Servants who steal the sugar.'"

At that, Mr. Ellison's lips curved upward. "Scandal and sugar?" He drew the book nearer, eyes gleaming. "By all means, let us have a look at once. Does he share his impressions of his great-nephew, I wonder? Or perhaps the parish vicar? Where shall we begin?"

"Oh, clergy," she said with a laugh, sliding her chair closer, their knees brushing without apology. "Always clergy."

The shadow between them had not vanished entirely, but in that moment, with the shared journal open, it had not won, either. They bent over the ancient little volume with its mousy leather and frayed spine, each laugh lightening the weight of the letter.

She was still laughing when she caught her breath enough to read aloud: "'Mr. Penny Pincher. Loud of voice. Thin of Soul.'"

She nearly toppled from her chair with the force of delight.

Graeme should not be watching her. He should not be aware of the way her eyes sparkled in the waning sun, the way a ribbon had loosened in her curls, or the way her sleeve grazed his shoulder because she had leaned just a fraction too close.

But he was.

He was utterly undone by the simplest of things: her laughter, her ease, her trust.

All that lingered of the letter was his own chagrin. How fortunate she was so forgiving.

She flipped a page. "And here... oh, no, this is truly wicked!" Voice choking, she read the line, "'Mrs. Smelling Salt is tragic of bonnet and overfond of the vicar.'"

He snorted. "Keep reading."

"'Lady L. dined today. Laughed like a duck. Is this a known and documented affliction?'"

That did it. She dropped her forehead to his shoulder, her own shaking with mirth.

Chuckling, he said, "If this is the earl's opinion of polite society, I begin to admire the man's notions." Reading further down the page, he said, "'Lord T. smells like an alehouse. T's sin is but little compared to Mrs. F., who stole my salt in belief I would not notice.' Let us hope, Miss Whittington, he has spared those of our own acquaintance."

Lifting her head, she tugged free her handkerchief to blot her eyes. "As curious as I am, I hope he never bothered. How dreadful to read the bare truth of the steward or poor Mrs. Redshaw! Do we really wish to know she pilfers the wine — "

"Or is overfond of chastisement," he finished for her.

"Oh, Mr. Ellison. This is a dangerous journal. And the worst of it? There are at least five more upstairs!"

As she dissolved into more laughter at the gossip five more must hold, he startled himself with the desire to clasp her hand, to press his lips against her knuckles. Instead, he stared, caught between awareness and longing.

More soberly than he had intended, he asked, "Is life so diverting, or is it only so when you're beside me?"

Her smile dipped as a pucker wrinkled her brow. She searched his face, although he did not know what she sought.

Her gaze lingered seconds too long, long enough for her cheeks to flush red and the air between them to shift, not merely with amusement but with something more fragile, and infinitely more volatile.

Looking down, she fidgeted with her handkerchief, fluster replacing her usual confidence. Abruptly, she rose. "Perhaps tomorrow we will see if his lordship has kinder things to say about his neighbors."

"Or we'll learn they all quack like ducks."

With a playful curtsy but hesitant smile, she left the study. Graeme watched her go, journal still in his hand, empty teapot on tray.

Alone again, Graeme let the journal fall shut. Her laughter echoed in his thoughts, light as a bell, warm as sunlight. He had waded into forbidden waters. Somewhere along the way, he had begun to long for her trust more than he feared her betrayal. And that, he suspected, made him the most vulnerable man in Lobelia Hall.

Chapter 12

Graeme fastened the last button of his waistcoat, the fine wool snapping into neat alignment beneath his fingers. The garment fit well, disconcertingly well. Tailored before he had left London, the riding kit had struck him then as an unnecessary extravagance. Now, as the morning light washed over the mirror, he hardly recognized the man in the reflection. The tailoring had been a wise choice, he decided.

The cut of the frock coat broadened his shoulders. The crisp linen at his throat framed his jaw rather than concealing it. Even the dark hue of the breeches seemed designed to lengthen his stride, to give him the look of a man with purpose, not a clerk hoping to blend into woodwork and wallpaper.

He exhaled slowly.

No one sees a drab clerk, he reminded himself. *No one questions a forgettable man.* That anonymity had made his disguise easy.

But this? This was something else entirely.

He pulled on his riding gloves, tightening each finger with deliberate precision. The weight of the leather felt like a decision, like an inevitability finally stepping into its own shape. Three weeks ago, he had feared failure so acutely he could hardly look the housekeeper in the eye. Three weeks ago, he had told himself he needed time to learn, to observe, to hide until he had matured into a man capable of the task before him.

But something had changed. Yesterday's laughter in the study. The brush of Miss Whittington's shoulder. The way she had looked at him as if he were *more* than a clerk, more than a wary pretender.

He squared his shoulders, studying the man in the glass again.

Imposter, whispered the part of him that still trembled.

Not for long, answered something steadier, something startlingly close to confidence.

He dragged a thumb across each waistcoat button, one at a time, half-amused, half-unsettled. He had accused *her* of being an imposter, of weaving falsehoods for advantage... but she had been the one to tell the truth. And he... *he* had been the one hiding behind a borrowed name, a borrowed role, a borrowed life until he could muster the courage to claim his own.

He gave his gloves a final tug and stepped away from the mirror. The air felt clearer, his pulse calmer. Yes. He could carry this presence. He could step into it fully when the time came.

Let today mark a beginning.

Even if it was only the beginning of a morning ride. All the rest of what that beginning entailed would keep for a while longer.

And if Miss Whittington looked at him twice... well, who could fault a man for taking pleasure where he found it? He desired to be a man worth her notice.

With a quiet breath of resolve, Graeme strode into the corridor, boots striking the polished floor with a confidence he had never quite allowed himself before. He took the circuitous route today, through the gallery and past the portraits of the stony-faced ancestors of the Earl of Collumby. This time, he did not flinch under their gaze.

Down the stairs, at last, he reached the study door and paused, noting the thin glow of morning sunlight shimmering beneath it. He was late. She would be inside already.

He allowed himself a private smile.

Good.

Let her see him on his own terms.

He pushed open the door.

Phoebe looked up from the journal, expecting to see Mr. Ellison in the doorway.

She did *not* expect… *this.*

She nearly dropped the book. For one wild heartbeat, she feared the Earl of Collumby had arrived at last, sweeping into his study unannounced, catching her surrounded by his late great-uncle's possessions, his solicitor nowhere in sight to present her properly.

But her second thought, louder, breathier, far less proper, was simply, *good heavens.*

The man in the doorway was a vision carved from every forbidden daydream she had ever denied herself. Tailored riding raiment hugged broad shoulders and long lines. Sunlight glinted off dark hair swept forward

in the fashionable London style. Confidence rolled off
him in a lazy, masculine wave. He carried his beaver hat
and riding crop with the casual authority of a man who
owned the world and expected it to applaud his arrival.

Her pulse fluttered. Her thoughts tangled.

Too soon for the earl to arrive. Far too soon!

And yet… this was the sort of man for whom
the heart — not the polite, well-behaved kind, but the
reckless one — dared beat.

He stepped closer, and she drew a sharp breath.
Taller than Mr. Ellison. Broader. Smiling a slow, devastating smile that curved across his mouth like sin.

Then he spoke, and her stomach dropped.

"The morning is far too fine to waste inside, don't
you think? Let all tedious matters go hang. We're
riding today, Miss Whittington."

She stared.

She blinked.

She made a noise that sounded dangerously
like *meep*.

Her mouth opened, closed, opened again. "I…
you… *Mr. Ellison*?"

His brows lifted in mock injury. "Were you
expecting someone else? Pray, name him, and I shall
know whom to challenge."

She tried to laugh. What escaped was a squeak
better suited to a frightened dormouse.

"You brought a riding habit," he went on
smoothly. "I trust?"

She nodded. Or rather, her entire head bobbed
like a carriage on a broken axle.

"Excellent. Hurry." He tipped his hat towards
her. "I'll have the horses brought around."

Phoebe realized only after he left that she was still clutching the journal to her chest like a shield. With a strangled sound, she flung it onto the table and dashed out the door. She made it halfway up the stairs before remembering, with dawning horror, that she had left her poor lady's maid sitting alone in the study, watching all of this unfold.

Breathless, Phoebe hurried down the stairs, curls askew from speed rather than vanity, rehearsing, desperately, one clever quip after another. *Anything* to prove she was not undone by whatever transformation Mr. Ellison had wrought upon himself.

At the last step before the door, she forced herself to stop.

Smooth your skirts. Chin up. Shoulders back. Do not *burst out this door like an overeager green girl.*

Only when her breath steadied did she walk through the open front door.

Sunlight spilled across the gravel drive and across *him.*

Mr. Ellison stood beside two saddled horses, crop resting with unstudied ease against his shoulder. The grooms lingered discreetly, but Phoebe scarcely noticed them. All her attention was arrested by the man who turned at the sound of her steps.

He smiled, slowly, knowingly, devastatingly.

She sucked in a breath.

Her knees, the traitors, trembled.

Do not *make a cake of yourself, Phoebe Whittington! This is still Mr. Ellison, even if he appears quite something* more *today*.

"Ah, perfect timing," he greeted. "I was beginning to fear the morning would grow jealous of your absence."

All five of her cleverly rehearsed replies flew through the nearest window.

"You... look... very..." She flailed. "Very present-able... for a morning of clerical correspondences."

In true Mr. Ellison fashion, his tone remained perfectly, mercilessly deadpan. "A dreadful meeting was expected with one of the gentleman tenants. I felt obliged to appear as though I knew what I was doing." Then, almost as an afterthought, he added, "But he is delayed. Seemed a sin to waste such a morning indoors."

Sin. Appropriate choice, for her thoughts were nearly indecent.

A gesture towards the horses. "Come. We are ready to ride, Miss Whittington."

Phoebe blinked and echoed faintly, "We... are?"

"You did change into your riding habit." His gaze glinted with amusement.

"Well... yes, I did," she said, lifting her chin with manufactured confidence, her words half bravado, half terror.

She stepped towards the nearest horse — one monstrously too large.

The horse snorted.

Phoebe tripped backwards.

Do not embarrass yourself.

She narrowed her eyes at the horse and, purely on impulse, snorted back.

Mr. Ellison's shoulders shook with suppressed mirth.

With the haughtiest toss of her curls she could manage, she reached for the side saddle's pommel, or what she *hoped* was the pommel, and lifted her foot towards the stirrup, realizing, too late, that this was entirely the wrong angle, and far too high besides.

A low voice intervened. "Allow me."

He stepped closer, cupping his hands to form a supportive step.

She attempted to locate his hands with her boot, slipped, and lurched backwards. His arm shot out, steadying her with confident strength.

"I assure you," she said, breathless, "I know perfectly well how to mount a horse."

His mouth quirked, delight unmistakable. "I will applaud you once you are successfully *on* the horse."

She glared.

He did not repent.

With infuriating competence, he set his hands gently, but firmly, at her waist, lifted her as though she weighed nothing at all, and settled her onto the saddle before she could marshal a single objection.

Her breath caught.

Her cheeks flushed.

Her pulse fluttered.

He adjusted her stirrup, guiding her foot into place, then stepped close enough for his voice to tickle warmly against her skin. "I believe," he said, eyes flicking up to meet hers, "the horse approves." Rather than await her response, Mr. Ellison mounted his horse with fluid and infuriating ease, the movement so simple, so elegant, and *so* masculine. "Ready?"

"Entirely," she lied.

With regal bravado, as though confidence alone could compensate for the fact she had no earthly idea what came next, she nudged her heel into the horse's side, just as she had read fashionable heroines do in novels.

The horse blew indignantly from its nostrils and stood absolutely still.

She nudged again, more firmly.

The horse took several leisurely steps. *Sideways.* Straight towards a shrub on the edge of the drive. Startled, Phoebe jerked the reins.

Mr. Ellison coughed, a cough which sounded suspiciously like a concealed laugh. "Oh dear," he said. "He favors the scenic route."

Phoebe yanked the reins several times, trying to guide the horse in the opposite direction. No effect. "He is *mocking* me."

"He is merely introducing himself." Mr. Ellison's lips twitched.

"I'll not be taken off my guard by his impropriety," she said with a sniff.

Shooting her riding companion a fiery look, which only seemed to delight him further, she tried another tug of the reins. The horse took another step, this time veering directly into the yew.

Whispering fiercely at the horse, she dug in her heels. "Oh heavens, no, no, stop, stop at once." Then, to Mr. Ellison, "He *is* mocking me."

"Undoubtedly. Though in his defense, he is in excellent company." He dipped his head and offered stewardly patience. "Perhaps a gentler pressure of the reins. Not so tight. Think of *guiding*, not wrestling." Effortlessly, he walked his horse alongside hers.

"I am *not* wrestling."

Her horse began nibbling at the yew.

"Of course not." His smile was too knowing to be legal.

After her light *suggestion* of the reins, her horse walked backwards. Mr. Ellison choked on a laugh.

Through gritted teeth, she asked, "Is my horse defective?"

"Only in the sense that he has already discerned your... spirited philosophy of leadership."

"I have no such philosophy."

"Precisely."

Her glare deepened, as did his grin.

After far more time than she would admit to any living soul, she, at last, managed to coax the obstinate horse into a reliable walk. So pleased at this small victory, she did not deny herself a triumphant smile, one that played on her lips as they followed the drive to the edge of the lawn, then cut across the estate, destination unknown.

The sedate walk was soon followed by a respectable trot, not at Phoebe's urging, but to her delight. Respectable, that was, until the animal surged into a *brisk* trot, jolting her about in the saddle, then, finding that pace too boring, quickened into a jostling canter. With a yelp, Phoebe pitched backwards in her saddle, grasping the reins for dear life.

Beside her in an instant, Mr. Ellison matched pace. "Easy, easy," he murmured, reaching across the narrow space to steady her reins with one practiced hand. "Don't fight him. Steady now."

She leaned instinctively towards him, the horses moving parallel as though choreographed. Every step brought her shoulder closer to his, every heartbeat louder in her ears.

"You're safe," he reassured, voice low enough to shiver down her spine. "Trust him. Trust yourself."

His touch guided hers, gentling the tension. She loosened her grip. The horse's gait settled beneath her.

"I..." She inhaled shakily. "I may have wanted too much too soon."

His smile softened, the teasing warmth replaced by something quieter, deeper. "There's no shame in wanting more. But you needn't grab it all at once."

Their eyes met, his steady and hers uncertain, and for a moment, it felt as though the sunlight caught between them, suspended.

Then the horse flicked an ear and snorted, impatient with the pause.

Phoebe tensed again.

Mr. Ellison's hand remained over hers a beat longer than necessary before he released her reins. "Shall we try again?"

They fell into an easier rhythm; her horse was either obedient now or humoring her.

"That's it exactly," he congratulated after they rounded an ornamental pond. "He answers with confidence. As I suspect, do you?"

She braved a glance, despite knowing her cheeks were flushed and curls wind-stirred beneath her bonnet. "Are you always this competent a rider?" Her tone demanded, but her voice held far less fire than she commanded.

Straight-faced, he replied, "So I've been told... by horses."

She laughed aloud, suddenly more amused by him than fearful of the horse.

They rode farther, the land opening into rolling green, the wind lifting the hem of her habit train and teasing stray curls across her cheeks.

The freedom of riding, from the height to the movement, sent a wild joy through her chest. It had nothing to do with his proximity, or so she tried to remind herself every few minutes.

"I see why people adore riding," she admitted. "It feels like... permission."

He turned to her, arching an eyebrow. "Permission to what?"

"To want things," she said before she could stop herself. "To chase something simply because it's beautiful."

His expression shifted with something tender, something vulnerable, but she could not understand what it meant. He looked away towards the fields and said quietly, "Freedom looks different when you're responsible for the land beneath your feet."

She studied his profile. Did his responsibility as solicitor weigh so heavily? It must. He made decisions on behalf of the earl, yet did not have the guidance of the estate solicitor to know what decisions were best.

Before she could probe, he flashed her a rakish half-smile. "And in your case, Miss Whittington, freedom looks mostly like trying to throw yourself off that horse."

She gasped. "I am *not!*"

"You have nearly succeeded so often, I am certain it is intentional."

"Only once."

"Thrice."

She glared, but the smile tugging the corners of her mouth betrayed her. Dreadful man looked far too pleased with himself for ruffling her feathers. Try as she might to tuck away her smile, she could not, and gave into a hearty laugh, one he soon echoed.

Wind swept around them, carrying their laughter and possibility.

The morning was theirs.

"You never told me," she said casually, as though her heart were not trying to beat right out of her chest, "how a London tradesman became an accomplished horseman."

With a rueful smile, he said, "My father fancied himself a great man of business, which he was, and would woo clients and potential partners as often in their country stables as at the dining table. I spent half my boyhood in the paddocks, trying to stay out of trouble and out from underfoot, all while observing his strategies."

"Is horsemanship a persuasive skill in business?" Her question teased, but he answered in earnest.

"One learns much about a man by the way he handles a horse. Patience. Restraint. Cruelty. Pride. Some men wield the whip at the slightest challenge, while others let the horse do as it pleases. But those worth trusting…" His eyes flicked to hers. "…know partnership."

Stealing a glance at the limp ribbons in her hands, she muttered, "Heaven help me. What must *my* horsemanship say about *me*?"

He angled her a look of disarming warmth. "That you are braver than you know and more determined than is wise."

"Is that a warning or a compliment?"

"Both," he said.

She stuttered a laugh, her breath tangling somewhere in her throat. "Papa has a barouche. I… I never learned to ride." The confession cost her an ounce of pride, although she suspected Mr. Ellison had already assumed as much.

"You're a fast learner, Miss Whittington. And that *is* a compliment."

They rode on, sunlight warming her shoulders. The landscape unfurled around them: gentle hills, fields of soft green, a wooded path dappled in lacework shadows. She relaxed enough to savor the ride and the company. Shropshire was far more beautiful than she had anticipated, as was, more specifically, the Lobelia Hall grounds. How fortunate she was to be here.

When they were once more in sight of the manor, he turned towards her with open admiration. She felt something in her shift, quietly, irrevocably.

"You see?" he said. "You and the horse understand each other now."

"He understands me entirely," she agreed. "I've simply chosen not to admit my dependence."

Chuckling, Mr. Ellison acknowledged, "An admirable strategy."

They slowed as they approached the gravel drive.

Softly, she said, "It is beautiful."

"Yes, very beautiful."

Something in his tone had her turning to him only to realize he was not looking at the scenery at all.

A little too loudly, she said, "You were right. It would have been a sin to stay indoors today."

"We should thank providence, it's only Saturday. Tomorrow would trap us in chapel instead."

She laughed but was all too aware of how life-altering had been last Sunday's service. Her pulse did not return to normal even as the gentle rhythm of the hooves carried them to the hall's entrance.

Chapter 13

Graeme sat alone in the study, the Monday morning sun only beginning to warm the windowpanes. The journal lay open before him, the ink faded in places, but unmistakably the late earl's hand. His intention had not been to read the journal without Miss Whittington, only to move it from the desk before she arrived, but an idle glance had drawn him in, urging his impulse to read one page… then another.

Until a line read:

My little P.W. was in my thoughts again this morning.

A cold thread wound through him.

He read the line twice more, as though repetition might rearrange the letters into something sensible. But no… they stood, stark and unyielding: *P.W.*

He sat back, pulse quickening, and let his eyes skim the next lines.

She is the brightness in my dusty tomb. I must provide for her.

Graeme swallowed. This was no legal phrasing, no dispassionate bequest. This was… affection, deep and personal. But *for whom*? No surname, no description of age or circumstance, no likeness or connection.

And Miss Phoebe Whittington had sworn she had never corresponded with the man.

He believed her.

Whether the earl had written some romanticized invention of her, or someone else entirely, needled at him, namely, the not knowing. He *could* question the codicil witnesses. Until recently, he had been so sure the P.W. was Miss Whittington. Who was to say the witnesses knew differently? No, he did not wish to involve others, not unless it became necessary. For now, the answer seemed to lie in the earl's own writing.

A soft knock interrupted his thoughts. He marked the page and closed the journal.

"Come," he called, hoping his voice did not betray his restlessness.

Miss Whittington stepped in with her maid trailing behind, sunlight following her into the room. She carried herself with a new kind of radiance, the echo of their ride still shimmering through her, softened now into something warm and quiet and irresistible.

Brightness in a dusty tomb, he thought, unprepared for the line to take on new meaning.

"Good morning, Mr. Ellison." Her smile tugged at unguarded emotions inside him. "Fanny insisted I not rush my hair today. I fear she will resign if I appear wind-tossed again."

From behind her, Miss Greeley mumbled something about *despairing*, not *resigning*.

Miss Whittington laughed, a lighter sound than the unexpected storm he could faintly hear gathering outside. "See? A tyrant of propriety."

Despite the weight on his mind, Graeme's mouth curved.

Her gaze flicked to the journal still in his hands. "You started without me!"

"Only a few pages. I meant to tidy, but temptation proved stronger than order today."

She claimed her usual chair with the careless grace of someone who belonged in a place she did not realize she belonged. The maid settled near the window with her mending.

"And what judgments of society has he rendered this morning?" Miss Whittington teased, reaching as though to snatch the journal from him. "Has he written of Mrs. Duck-Laugh again?"

He hesitated. Only for a heartbeat, but it was a beat too long.

Her smile faded. "Is something wrong?"

Her eyes asked a quieter question: *Did another letter about me arrive?*

Graeme drew a steadying breath and slid the journal towards her, opening to the marked page as he took his seat. "Perhaps you should read this entry."

Her brows knit as she leaned in. She traced the lines with her fingertips until... bewilderment, not recognition, formed her features.

"P.W.," she murmured. Then, almost absently, "Oh! Those are my initials."

She did not tense.

She did not pale.

She did not look away.

Instead, she tipped her head in puzzlement. "I cannot decide whether to be flattered or alarmed. Why would he write about me?"

"You... never knew him," Graeme asserted gently. "Not personally."

"No." Her fingertips brushed the page. "My father corresponded, as I told you, but I did not. Perhaps... perhaps he wrote these while thinking of my father's letters... in anticipation of my arrival? Then, he's overly fond of cryptic abbreviations, as we've discovered; this could refer to anyone." After taking a quiet moment to think, she offered with a broadening grin, "What if he writes about Prudence Warren! Or Poppy White? Oh! I know! Prunella Wiggensworth, shepherdess extraordinaire!"

Graeme barked a laugh, which dislodged much of the tension that tightened his chest. The names were absurd, as there were no such people.

"Whatever the case," she continued, "he was a lonely man with a penchant for gossip and invented companions. This P.W. may have existed solely in his imagination."

"But he wrote of ensuring her welfare," he pressed, keeping his tone neutral. "That suggests someone real."

"Then he was sentimental and besotted with the fair-haired Prunella. Shepherdesses have been known to inspire poetic devotion."

From her perch near the window, Miss Greeley made a noise suspiciously close to a smothered giggle.

Graeme ignored her. Instead, he watched Miss Whittington, seeing only the sincerity of her confusion and the openness of her expression. There was no guile, no hint of calculation, no questions or curiosities of promised provisions. If she *were* the P.W. of the codicil, the bequest had been the earl's whim, not her ambition.

He found himself studying the curve of her face, the warmth in her eyes, the ease with which she met uncertainty and refused to let fear or vanity cloud her honesty.

How curious it must be for her to read initials so familiar yet have no notion whether the earl had written about the young bride he hoped for, or some other creature entirely: a lost love, a married woman for whom he pined, a favorite hound.

"Fanny," Miss Whittington said suddenly, "be a dear and fetch the next volume. Upstairs parlor, third shelf on the right." For Graeme, she flashed a mischievous smile. "Perhaps he's embellished about our mysterious Prunella in the next journal!"

Although Miss Greeley rose, she held none of her mistress's enthusiasm. Wringing her hands, her apprehension overshadowing her obedience, she hesitated. "Miss… ought I?" Lowering her voice with a flick of her gaze to Graeme, she added, "I would never wish to be accused of snooping…."

Graeme nodded reassuringly. "You have my permission. Nothing in this house is forbidden to our most honored guest."

Relieved, the maid curtsied and hurried out.

Before Miss Whittington could speak again, thunder cracked low and rolling, ominously close, shaking the glass in its lead.

They both jumped.

Only then did Graeme realize how much the light had dimmed. He crossed to the window as the sky darkened from blue to brooding slate. "A storm is nearly upon us."

As if his words heralded the uninvited guest, a blast of wind rattled the casements. A sheet of rain slapped through an open window, splashing across the rug.

Miss Whittington shrieked, a hand flying to her mouth. "Oh, Mr. Ellison!"

Graeme lunged forward. "Stand back —"

But another gust swept into the room before he reached it, sending loose papers swirling across the floor. Rain pattered across the floorboards, catching several pages before he could rescue them.

Miss Whittington darted after scattered sheets, breathless with laughter. "What a wicked storm."

He secured one window, then another. A gale beat at the house, determined to gain admittance. As another *whoosh* surged, Miss Whittington abandoned the airborne papers and rushed to help latch the remaining casements.

At the second window, she gasped, "This one is stuck!"

Rain sprayed through the opening. She let out a startled little laugh as droplets hit her sleeve.

Gallantly, Graeme reached her in three strides. "Allow me?"

She stepped aside, but not quickly enough to avoid another scatter of rain across her hair and cheek. She ducked behind him in a half-instinctive, half-delighted motion that sent his pulse skittering.

He tugged at the window. The hinge was stuck, unmoving. The wind drove the rain harder with every attempt to tug the window closed. At last, he worked the iron free, coaxing the blasted thing into submission, just as a gust shoved at the frame, forcing the window shut with a violent thud and knocking him backwards.

Straight into her.

She caught at his shoulders to keep from falling. He pivoted, wrapping an arm around her waist to steady her.

They froze.

Her breath feathered against his throat.

Her curls grazed his cheek.

Her body aligned with his as though shaped for his embrace.

Miss Whittington cleared her throat softly, stepping back with visible reluctance. "What an undignified battle... with the window," she said, color rising to her cheeks.

Graeme found his voice, though roughened. "The window was no match for us. It surrendered once it saw how formidable were its opponents."

Thunder rolled again.

She shivered.

Without hesitation, he slipped off his coat and draped it around her shoulders. "Here. Summer storm or not, you're chilled."

When she looked up at him, truly looked, her expression stirred something tender between them, soft as a breath but twice as dangerous.

"Thank you," she whispered.

He swallowed, unable to summon a proper reply.

Lightning flashed. Rain pummeled the glass.

Clutching his coat close, Miss Whittington glanced back at the journal still open on the desk. "Perhaps we should read only the less tumultuous pages today."

"Perhaps." His smile teased.

It had only been a storm. It had only been two initials. But everything had changed. He knew it as surely as he knew his own name.

Not because of the storm.

Not because of the initials.

Because of her.

Because she had trusted him. Because she had chosen truth when evasion would have served her better. Because she stood before him, wrapped in his coat, cheeks flushed, unaware of the hold she already had on him.

And because he was perilously close to wanting what he had no right to want.

The storm worsened with every passing minute. Thunder cracked. Wind moaned. Rain lashed the windows in wild, relentless sheets.

At last, the study door flew open, and for one heart-pounding instant, Graeme thought the storm had forced its way inside. But it was only Miss Greeley.

She clutched something to her chest, eyes round with terror. "That's no ordinary storm. That's judgment, that is!"

Miss Whittington stifled a laugh. Graeme did not dare look at her, not when his coat still wrapped around her shoulders, not when he could still feel the echo of her pressed against him.

The maid thrust her prize towards her mistress. "I found these tucked behind the books, miss." Triumphantly, she added, "They are addressed to you, so I thought you'd want them at once."

Miss Whittington's smile slipped. "Addressed to me? Fanny, that makes no sense."

"But... but it says so right here." She freed a letter from the bundle with fumbling fingers. "P.W. Exactly as your mother named you."

"Fanny, those are not… those cannot — "

"Perhaps Prunella again?" Graeme offered, hoping to coax a smile. But Miss Whittington's gaze remained fixed on the letters, troubled and disbelieving.

He approached the maid. "May I?"

She surrendered them with visible relief.

Thunder boomed overhead, shaking the glass. Another gust tore at the house, wrenching open the latch on the window where the maid had been sitting before her errand.

"Oh no!" she shrieked as rain slapped through the opening, soaking her chair. Unlike her mistress, she did not find the storm amusing. She bolted for the door. "Towels! I'll fetch towels!" Her hem caught around her ankles; she barely recovered herself with a squeak before disappearing into the antechamber.

Pressing a hand to her lips to stifle another laugh, Miss Whittington said, "Poor Fanny."

Graeme allowed himself a smile, realizing too late in his distraction that the maid had left the window open. Another surge of wind blasted inside, whipping the papers they had only just saved back into chaos. Setting the letters on the table, he lurched for the window as Miss Whittington dove for the scattered pages yet again.

"Hurry," she called, a bit too gleeful for the occasion, hardly sounding as though she wanted anything hurried at all.

He latched the window with a decisive click and turned back to find her kneeling on the floor, curls tumbled, cheeks pink. The sight of her there, unguarded and joyful, tugged at something deep in him.

He joined her, crouching beside her as she gathered pages into little piles. A damp curl clung to her temple; she pushed it back with an impatient huff.

"Here… before these become puddle-paper." Her voice tangled with mischief.

He carried her stacks to the desk, retrieved the remaining sheets, and returned far sooner than he wished. Too soon, they were idle again, alone with the journal, the storm, and the small bundle of letters waiting on the table. He settled into the chair, eyes drawn to the twine-tied packet. Only a handful of letters. Neatly bundled.

Freeing the twine, he let the letters tumble between them.

"What have we found?" She poked at the pile, wary.

Their hands reached towards the same letter and brushed. Heat shot through him at the contact, sharp, immediate, impossible to ignore. She did not withdraw. A faint blush bloomed across the bridge of her nose, but she continued sifting through the letters.

Each was marked only with:

To P.W.

Miss Whittington inhaled sharply. "They *cannot* be for me. Can they?" She lifted one letter after another at random.

Graeme chose one with careful fingers. The paper was crisp, unworn, unsent. "No fraying," he murmured. "The wax remains intact. These were never posted."

"Why would he write to me but never send them?"

"I cannot say," he admitted in a low voice, his thoughts churning.

They both stared at the pile. Then at each other. Then back again.

Thunder rippled. The room dimmed. Lightning flickered across her face, enchanting and ghostly all at once. Rising, Graeme crossed to the desk for the tinderbox, striking steel to flint until the cloth caught so he could light the wick.

The candle cast restless shadows.

Watching the flame glow, Miss Whittington repeated, "*Why* write letters but never send them? *Why* keep them hidden away?"

He had no answer.

She held one of the letters closer. "And this — this one is like the journal entry: 'my little P.W.' It feels so… possessive." She shuddered, the earlier laughter replaced by pinched brows. "I do not know whether it should frighten me."

Graeme felt a primal urge to shield her from that fear. "Phoebe, I—"

He stopped. Her given name had slipped out, natural as breathing.

Her gaze snapped to his, startled.

Before either could react to his uninvited familiarity, the maid crashed back into the room.

"Towels! I have towels!"

Miss Whittington jolted from her thoughts, clutching his coat tighter with one hand and an unopened letter with the other.

And just like that, the spell of the moment fractured, but the weight of it lingered, heavy as the storm clouds outside.

The door had barely closed before Graeme exhaled his pinned emotions. He pressed both palms against the desk. Her scent lingered on his coat, orange blossoms and rain, and the memory of her soft against him during their brief embrace hit him with far more force than the storm had.

He sank into the chair, raking a hand through his hair.

What had happened?

The room remained in mild disarray. Papers lay drying across the desk. Towels lined several windows like soldiers on parade. The candle guttered. Rain tapped an uneven rhythm against the windows. He forced himself to move, to collect pages, straighten stacks, occupy his hands because his mind refused to steady.

Her laughter clung to the air.

Her warmth pressed phantom-soft against his chest.

He pulled open the drawer and looked at the bundle of letters he had tucked inside. *To P.W.* He had not imagined her bewilderment. There had been no guile, only confusion, concern, and that spark of humor she used to fend off discomfort. She had not known the earl. Instinctively, he knew she spoke the truth. But the letters… they were something he could not ignore, not with the codicil an ever-pressing obstacle.

He closed the drawer.

More pressing, far more unsettling, was the realization blooming slow and hot in his chest: *he wanted her.*

Not as a suspect.

Not as a responsibility.

Not as an obligation handed down by an earl's dying whim.

He wanted *her*.

Her wit, her light, her impossible reliance, and yes, her touch.

He swallowed.

The codicil now felt like a stone in his pocket rather than a weapon. He needed time, time to understand what the letters meant, time to understand what *she* meant to him, time before telling her anything that might send her running from the hall—and from him. Not because he wished to trap her, but because—

He inhaled shakily.

He simply was not ready to let her go, not before they had a chance together.

He stood and crossed to a window, staring out at the last fragments of the storm. The rain had softened to a thin silver mist. Irrationally, foolishly, he hoped she would return later, as she had the afternoon she discovered the journals. If only to ask about the letters. If only to sit near him again. If only to look at him with those wide, bold eyes and ask—

What happens next?

He did not know. But he wanted to find out.

Phoebe dismissed Fanny the moment they reached her chamber. Poor Fanny looked ready to write an outraged report to the Almighty about storms, puddles, and dripping papers.

Once the door closed, quiet finally settled. She leaned back against the wood, breath catching. The memory of his coat still hung about her shoulders, heavy with rain and warmth, with the essence of him. She breathed in the scents of cedar, soap, and something alluring and unmistakably him. Her pulse leapt.

What is happening to me?

She crossed to the window. The storm clouds were thinning, light breaking through in pale, shy patches. She pressed her fingertips to the glass, remembering the moment the window had slammed shut, sending him stumbling backwards into her.

Then his arms had come around her.

His breath had tickled her cheek.

The way he held her… instinctively, gently, protectively, as though she mattered.

Her heart thudded.

She should change out of her damp gown. She should ring for tea. She should do anything except stand there, holding her breath like a green girl fresh from her first ball. But she could not stop remembering the moment.

Thoughts of the letters and the journal intruded, unwanted. She could not stop thinking about them either.

My Little P.W.

The words unsettled her… but not as much as the thought of what Mr. Ellison must think. She hoped — more desperately than she wished to admit — that he believed her, that he did not imagine her exchanging secret missives with the late earl.

What must he think of her?

This morning, he had returned to the self-contained clerk she knew so well, yet she could no longer see him as a stiff and unsmiling guardian of duty, not after their ride. Now, she saw a strong, decisive, and masculine man. At no point in her life had she ever felt so safe and so vulnerable all at once.

Pacing the room, she struggled to settle, to calm. Every part of her felt *alive* from his embrace.

He had looked at her differently today, not like a clerk scolding a troublesome guest, or as a man burdened with responsibility, rather he looked at her as if he *saw* her. As if he could see straight through the armor she polished daily: charm, wit, varnished confidence. He had stood with her at the window, his breath steady and close, and she had felt...

Safe.

Exposed.

Seen.

Pressing a hand to her warm cheek, she whispered to the empty room, "What am I doing?"

She wanted to see him again. Tonight. Tomorrow. After all she had been through, she was not ready for desire. It was far too terrifying, too unsettling, but curse it, she wanted, and that want felt wonderful.

Crawling onto the bed, still dressed in her damp gown, she closed her eyes. After dinner... was that too soon? Too desperate? She could... *yes*... she could ask him if they might read one of the letters. That was a believable excuse. Would he be in the study after dinner or, better yet, after supper, the cover of evening far more to her advantage? She aimed to find out.

Chapter 14

The drizzle tapped impatiently at the window. Fanny had long since retired, leaving Phoebe to pretend to read, pretend to embroider, pretend to breathe like a rational creature. When pretending had outworn its welcome, she tried brushing her hair, straightening the room, even praying for composure. Nothing helped. Nothing quieted her pulse. Nothing softened the memory of his arms around her. *He had only caught you from falling, silly goose – little more than a trifle!*

With a huff, she snatched up a taper and lit it with the mantel candelabra, the tiny flame trembling as though complicit in her impropriety.

"Just one letter," she whispered to herself. "One. And then I shall sleep."

But of course, her desire had nothing to do with reading letters.

She slipped into the corridor. The manor was dark and full of echoes: low moans of wind buffeted through chimneys, the hiss of rain dying against mullioned windows and stone. She hastened her steps, eyes darting from one shadow to another, willing the doors to remain closed and her movements to haunt in ghostly silence.

By the time she reached the study door, her heart had lodged in her throat. A hand to her hair reassured it was still coiffed. A smoothing palm to her gown affirmed she had not wrinkled the muslin with impatience. A touch to her feverish cheek confirmed she must be terribly flushed.

She raised her hand to knock. Hesitated. Lowered it again.

Foolish girl. He does not live *in the study. Why would he be here so late into the evening?*

Sensibility teased that he may have lingered in hope she would arrive with tea as she had done before. Sense replied it was no longer afternoon. All in the house were abed. No woman would *dare*, not so late into the evening. He must have retired long ago, either because he did not expect her at all or because he had quite given up any hope of her returning.

With that, her confidence soared that he would not answer, and she could retreat to her bedchamber like a sensible creature.

She raised her hand to knock. Hesitated. Knocked.

Almost at once, before her hand fell back to her side, the door opened.

The dark antechamber in which she waited, illuminated only by the bruised blue of her taper, brightened, bathed in a fiery glow as the warmth from within swallowed the shadows. Framed by the doorway, basked in a golden halo of candleflames, stood Mr. Ellison, coat off and shirtsleeves rolled to his elbows.

Their eyes met, and she saw in his expression neither disapproval nor surprise, but rather an inquisitive, nay, *affectionate* welcome. *He* had *been waiting for me.*

"Miss Whittington..." His voice was deeper than usual, resonant, intimate. "Is everything... are you well?"

She swallowed. "I... yes. I am well."

Neither moved. Neither spoke. Their gazes tangled.

"I cannot stop thinking about..." Afraid she would lose her courage, she finished in a rush, "the letters."

His brows notched.

How transparent the excuse! Her cheeks heated.

"The ones Fanny found," she clarified needlessly. "Not letters I have written or received because I have not written any, which is not to say I was expecting to receive letters, either, or that these letters..."

She let the madness trail as she inhaled a deep, shaky breath.

Better to stick to the plan than fling herself upon his person. Whatever he must think of her now, there was no retracting words or steps. "It would be terribly improper to open a letter not my own, more so to open one so late in the evening... but..." Her voice dropped. "I shall lose sleep and sense if I do not."

In his eyes, she saw a tumult of emotions — tenderness coupled with something far more dangerous.

"Improper..." he began, pausing as though first to taste the word, and then, on finding no objection to its spice, he continued, his gaze holding fast to hers, "Miss Whittington, if we cross the point of propriety, I am fully prepared to share the consequences."

Her heart pounded, wobbled, and nearly seized.

He stepped back, inviting her entry. She slipped inside, narrowly brushing past him, the scent of cedar, wax, and man enfolding her, the warmth of his person close enough to feel, dangerous enough to unsettle.

Candelabras framed the settee. Shadows stretched long across the floor, darkening the corners. His coat hung over the screen before the hearth, a reminder of their embrace. Her breath caught.

"Please," he said, gesturing to their usual table. "Sit."

She hesitated for one breath, then sat at the settee instead, setting her candlestick on the tea table. Although she did not look at Mr. Ellison to gauge his reaction—not with her chin raised, shoulders back, and confident composure in place, a woman who knew what she was about, in stark contrast to the sniveling maiden he had witnessed at the study door moments before—she was aware of his every movement. What she had not expected was for him to do exactly what she wished.

The settee cushion dipped next to her. He sat close enough that the edge of his sleeve whispered against her arm. Gooseflesh tickled across her skin.

"Thank you…" she said, "for seeing me."

His answering smile was quiet, sincere, almost undone. "There is nothing you could ask for that I would refuse."

Pit-pat, pit-pat, pit-pat answered her pulse.

Then she glanced back at the tea table. Piled next to an abandoned book he had left facedown were the unopened letters. He *had* been waiting for her!

But did he understand she had come for him, not the letters? She hoped he did. She hoped he did not. *Carry on with the charade, Phoebe, before you make a cake of yourself.*

"Just one," she said, her eyes on the letters.

"Just one."

They looked far more intimidating than they had earlier. She did *not* want to open them. What were they to her? The words of a stranger she had rejected and then finally accepted out of desperation. Nothing could be gained from this.

They both reached for the top letter, their hands grazing.

She retreated.

His hand hovered, a question awaiting an answer.

She nodded, heart pounding.

He chose a letter at random, then held it between them. For a moment, they both stared at it, neither moving to open it, neither speaking, both watching the candlelight quiver across the unyielding paper. Behind them, the rain tapped anxiously at the windows. The silence felt as fragile as glass, too easily shattered by spoken word.

Phoebe exhaled, slow, unsteady.

With a sweep of his thumb, Mr. Ellison broke the seal, the wax crackling. As the letter unfolded, they both leaned in, their shoulders nearly touching.

Outside, the storm sighed.

Inside, a tempest swelled.

Between them, the letter's edges unfurled. The candleflames leaned forward, straining towards the contents. Graeme angled the paper, uncertain whether he ought to read aloud or let her gather courage first.

A braved glance at her profile answered him: rather than read, she studied her folded hands, as though in search of fortitude.

He cleared his throat. "'Sunshine of my declining years,'" he began.

Miss Whittington choked on a startled laugh, her tone incredulous, her blush mortified. "Oh dear. He did not hold back, did he?"

"Apparently not." He continued, "'I think of no one except you. How cruel is life to keep us apart?'"

She snorted, amused but flustered. When he glimpsed the upcoming lines, he thought better of reading another word aloud. He handed her the letter. Their hands brushed. Neither withdrew.

Over her shoulder, he skimmed the shaky script. The letter was short but embarrassingly intimate. Her cheeks flushed as she read, and Graeme found himself torn between watching her reactions and deciphering more of the late earl's lyricism. Nothing in the letter was improper, merely… extravagant. So extravagant, he shifted on the settee, uneasy with the strange blend of envy and sympathy stirring in him.

He knew she had reached the end when she read aloud, "'You shall be well cared for, my beloved. If I cannot have you in life, then in death, I can leave you assurance.'" She folded the page with careful precision, pressing the creases as if to seal in the words. "I think one letter is enough for tonight."

"Quite enough," he agreed, his voice raspy.

She set the letter on the tea table and drew her hands back to her lap. "It is strange to think he wrote those things. Such… devotion."

"Stranger still," Graeme murmured, "to reconcile these sentiments with a man I understood only to be stern."

"Stern?" She looked up, astonished. "You are generous! He terrified me, if only from his portrait." Her lashes fluttered. "How wrong of me to mock him if *this* is how he felt. All this time, I thought he wanted a young bride, any young bride, to thwart his great-nephew. I never imagined he… imagined me into some sort of Madonna."

He angled his head sharply. "Miss Whittington, you owe the man nothing, least of all guilt."

"Perhaps not, but I *do* feel guilty. If he imagined me to be the creature he describes, then… well, I ought never to have rejected him, or accepted him, or *anything*. I am hardly 'sunshine,' Mr. Ellison. More like a badly-behaved lantern."

He chuckled, hoping his humor would wash over her like a balm.

Her answering smile flickered, then dimmed. "And yet… I admit I am relieved. There is an intensity about him, from portrait to poetry. There is *ownership* in his gaze, possession in his words. If he felt so strongly, I fear he would have tried to claim me, body and soul."

Without thought, he reached for her hand, threading his fingers through hers, the warmth of their palms heartening and sure. "You would not have been safe in such a marriage." His tone surprised him, protective and fierce.

She traced his knuckles with her fingertips. "Well, he clearly idealized her, whoever she was. No woman could live up to those expectations."

Bringing their joined fingers to his lips, he brushed the air above the back of her hand with a reverent kiss. "Some women could."

She laughed, a brittle little sound, and slipped her hand from his. "It reminds me of something absurd Papa used to say, more than once, I hasten to add. When I was around twelve, he hired a governess, poor woman, who tried desperately to teach me all the proper lady's accomplishments. Painting, piano-forte, poetry recitation… Oh, I was abysmal!"

"I doubt that."

"Oh no," she insisted. "I assure you, I was. Truly! My sketches looked penned by a foxed squirrel!"

He smiled where she expected him to laugh, but he did not interrupt, not when he recognized the wound beneath the humor.

"Whenever I showed Papa my progress," she continued, forcing merriment into her words, though her voice turned faint, "he would laugh and tell me not to fret about my failings. None of that mattered. My only real asset was my beauty, and I ought to learn to wield that instead of bothering with refinements I could never master. And he was quite right, you know! The governess was dismissed before long, and Papa took up my education. Men only ever want beauty or money, and for a time, I could offer both." Her smile crumpled.

Graeme's expression hardened. "That is untrue, as well as cruel."

With a lift of a single shoulder, she shrugged, as though her father's verdict weighed nothing at all. The ghost of a smile haunted as she looked up at him with glistening eyes. He read in them the hurt she tried to hide: her longing to be valued, her fear she never would be, her brave armor of brash humor. Desperately, he wanted to reclaim her hand. He restrained.

To steady her mood, he offered, "Since you paint like a squirrel, and I have never held a brush in earnest, perhaps we should disgrace ourselves together. Tomorrow?"

"*Painting*?"

Feigning solemnity, he nodded. "It is what people of quality do, I believe."

With a burst of laughter, returning more to herself, she insisted, "Neither of us is *quality*!"

"You know a marchioness," he countered. "This is more quality than I can boast; therefore, you are far more a person of quality than I, and so, I wish to learn vicariously through you what it takes to become such a learned personage."

Scoffing at his absurdities, she argued, "I hardly count the Marchioness of Pickering as *quality*. She was once my maid!" Mortified, she covered her mouth with her hand.

Graeme's curiosity sparked. "Was she indeed?" Then, with a roguish grin, he said, "Ah! So that is why you wish to meet the new earl. You fear Miss Greeley will steal him."

Just as he wished, she dissolved into helpless laughter, clutching his sleeve for balance. Once she regained herself with a dab of her kerchief to the corners of her eyes, her gaze drifted to meet his, and her hand slipped from his arm with palpable reluctance.

He caught it again, his thumb brushing her knuckles. "If you'd prefer a picnic instead…"

Thunder rolled an amused reply.

With a rueful smile, she teased, "And with my luck, sit in the mud?"

"Painting, then?"

"Painting."

Their hands lingered. He listened as her breath quickened, his pulse answering in kind.

The taper's flame flared.

Graeme leaned closer until he felt her breath against his cheek.

"The hour grows late," he said, huskier than intended, every fiber in him willing her to stay.

They rose together, fingers entwined, the hem of her gown whispering against his stockinged feet. The flame dipped, quivering, bowing beneath the weight of the moment. His gaze fell fleetingly, treacherously, to her parted lips.

He released her hand.

She stepped back.

"Goodnight, Phoebe."

A hitched breath.

"Goodnight…"

"Graeme."

"Goodnight, Graeme."

After two hesitations and three backwards glances over her shoulder, she slipped out the door, taking with her the candlestick and the last of his composure.

Dew jeweled every blade of grass as the sun crept through thinning clouds. The air smelled of earth and new beginnings, fresh, green, and alive. Phoebe paused at the path's bend, pressing a hand to her fluttering stomach. *It is only painting*, she told herself. *Painting and Mr. Ellison. Two harmless things. Three, perhaps, if one counts his smile.*

He stood beneath the linden tree ahead, sleeves rolled, coat draped over a bench, hair slightly tussled from the breeze, so reminiscent of last evening, her breath caught in her throat. A pair of easels waited beside him, along with brushes, small pots of pigment, porcelain palettes, and paper so pristine it seemed a crime she would soon ruin it.

When he saw her, his expression softened into something intimate, a private smile meant only for her.

"Good morning…." He drew out the greeting with long, flirty vowels.

"Good morning," her pulse skipped to add, "Graeme. I hope I have not kept you waiting."

"Not at all. I arrived only moments ago." The corners of his eyes crinkled. "I'm not too proud to admit I am relieved you came."

She felt the truth of it, settling like sunlight inside her chest. He offered her the better of the two brushes. She accepted it gingerly, glancing at the pigment pots.

"So," she began, "do we paint the garden? The manor? One another?"

"Let us begin modestly," he said gravely. "With… that leaf."

She squinted at the tree and its myriad leaves. "*That* one?"

"That one. I believe in challenging ourselves with a focus on detail."

In answer to his serious tone, she cast him a look of theatrical dread before preparing her brush for the first tentative stroke. At least she remembered enough of her instruction to know what to *do* with the brush and paint, even if the end result would be laughable at best.

True to form, after much concentration, much dipping of the brush, and much tongue wagging — literally in her case — what emerged upon her watercolor paper bore only the faintest resemblance to vegetation. More like something that had… well… perhaps fallen off a startled hedgehog rather than a tree.

Mr. Ellison, or Graeme, rather, tucked his twitching smile behind an expression of critical austerity. "It has… personality."

"Sir," she said, choking on laughter at both his reaction and her attempt at art, "it has *ailments*."

Unable to hide his own laughter any longer, he let it spill into the morning air. So low, warm, and utterly delightful, she felt herself lean towards him, drawn as a blossom seeks the sun.

"Shall we add a branch?" she asked with a flutter of lashes.

"Splendid notion. Let us not leave this lonely leaf alone on the page. A branch with brethren leaves to offer solidarity."

A glimpse of his watercolor inspired a smidge more confidence in her hedgehog-spined leaf. That was, until she attempted her next brushstroke. The handle slipped. Paint splashed across the paper with enthusiastic blots. She squeaked, trying not to drop the brush on her gown.

In a heartbeat, his hand closed around hers, rescuing the brush and steadying her nerves. Their fingers laced as he slid his smooth palm over the back of her hand to free her of the brush and set it with the paints until she could recover herself, mostly from laughter than from disaster, although after the feel of his caress, she rather thought she needed to recover from his proximity. They shared a breath before he withdrew back to his easel.

Phoebe clasped her hands, struggling to keep them from trembling. With patience she did not think she had, she waited for her cheeks to return to a believable shade of pale and for him to return his attention to his watercolor sheet.

And then, she blurted out, "I enjoy this. Being with you. You're the only person who has ever looked at me and seen... me. Not my father's daughter."

His brush stilled. Then, in a quiet but sure voice: "The feeling is mutual."

So much for pale cheeks.

He meant it. She could *feel* he meant it. No flattery. No calculation. Just truth. But then she had to wonder, if she were the only one to see *him* as he saw *her*, what did other people see him as, and how were they too near-sighted not to see *him*?

With renewed focus, she dipped her brush again.

One minute passed. Then two. Soon ten. And finally...

The result of her branch with brethren leaves was, somehow... worse than before.

"Oh dear." She fought a grin. "Papa was right. I'd best stick to being decorative."

His brows rose in objection.

"No need to look at me like that. I did warn you. I have but the one asset, and I should be wielding it rather than this brush." Tossing the stick with the paints in an overdramatized flourish, she posed prettily for her audience, giving her curls a little flounce and her brows a flirty waggle. "Paint me instead. Let the leaf envy my beauty."

Graeme — oh, how delicious to think of him as *Graeme*, which suited him far and away better than Mr. Ellison, a name that never fit him well, she did not think — coughed a laugh but was torn between scolding her with those pursed brows and admiring her with his roaming eyes. She let him stay in that delicious conflict as his gaze swept over her.

"I will never deny your beauty, dear Phoebe. I am but a man, and you know as well as I how captivating you are. Any man who would deny that fact is blind, a fool, or a liar. *But* on one point I must contest: you possess *far* more assets than beauty." He raised a staying hand. "Don't object, at least not until I've established credibility. For, you see, if you were *only* beautiful, my head would not be so easily turned."

"Oh, I *do* see." She harrumphed. "Having turned *your* head is a grand prize, then. Any other man would only want me for my raven curls and coquettish doe eyes."

"Coy. I would describe them as coy."

She snorted indelicately. "I should like to know what Papa would think of you. He sent me here to snare an earl. What would he say if I brought home a fellow tradesman turned solicitor?"

He stepped back, brows arching again. "Bring me home? I show you a kindness by inviting you into the garden to *paint*, and you now think I'm wrapped about your finger, a lovesick swain, counting flower petals in hopes you'll accept my proposal? You *are* bold, Miss Phoebe Whittington."

She stepped towards him with a sashay of her hips. "I could win your heart if I wanted."

"With what? Your crooked twig?" he motioned to her easel.

A sly smile and another step forward. "Magnetism."

He threw back his head and laughed. "Going to mesmerize me, then?"

With another harrumph, she crossed her arms. "You must be one of those men who is not swayed by beauty rather by money. Papa always said men lusted after one or the other. And Papa is always right."

She teased, of course, as she was enjoying their game, enjoying it immensely, and judging from his expression, he too was enlivened by the exchange.

"Yes," she continued, "I believe I shall leave a note of apology to the Earl of Collumby that he must find a new solicitor, at least for the interim, because I must abscond with his man of business."

"If you desire painting lessons, my dearest, you need only to ask." This time, he stepped forward, the space between them closing. "And what do you suppose your father would say should you present me as the preferred suitor over a newly inherited peer of the realm?"

"Whatever he says, he shall be right. He's always right, you see." With a satisfied smirk, she added the winning quip. "Not even Freddy could fool him."

And then her words dawned.

The world around her froze, as if even the leaves dared not rustle.

Her breath escaped in a whimper, taking with it the last of her resolve.

A hand cupped her elbow. She blinked.

"Allow me to guide you to the bench," said a distant voice, a tender voice that warmed the chill inside her. "Do you have any hartshorn with you? You look faint."

She hissed at the insinuation she needed smelling salts, but then realized she was still so stunned to have spoken *his* name allowed — and to Graeme! — she had not hissed after all, only wished too. The hand cupping her elbow held fast. *Please don't let me go.*

Without thinking, she reached to clasp his other hand, holding it as a lifeline. Graeme waited, silent and patient.

She inhaled.

She exhaled.

What was the point without trust? And so, she chose to trust him.

"What is beauty without sense?" she asked. "If you're even half as serious as you jest, you deserve to know the truth." Her voice wavered, but she pressed on. "About Freddy. About… about the elopement."

Phoebe took her time. Graeme did not press her, only squeezed her hand.

"Time is not an indicator of affection, I've learned. He courted me for some time. Freddy, that is. Only in secret, as Papa hated him and forbade him from seeing me, insisting he was a wastrel, a roué. But Freddy courted me with feverish persistence. For months."

If she thought she could share the tale with detached neutrality, she was mistaken. Every detail still stung, from his lies to her naivety. *Why* did Papa have to be right? She resented that most of all.

"I loved him. Foolishly. Entirely. I trusted him more than anyone. And he wanted... not me. Only the money I would bring." At least she did not cry. Curiously, her eyes remained dry, and the heartache she expected never squeezed. The sting was only the humiliation of gullibility. "He convinced me he neither needed nor wanted my dowry... claimed he would inherit a windfall, and that alone would sustain us, but I did not care, only that he swore to love me. I was *fool* enough to believe he loved me for me."

Her breath hitched.

"I was desperate to escape Papa. It would be a lie to say that did not sway me, but I believed so madly in true love then that I would have chosen the promise of love over a thousand aristocrats or purses of endless wealth."

Her throat closed around the memory.

"By the time I realized he had lied, everything was already lost. Reputation. Dowry. Friends. Even myself, I suppose." With a dry laugh, she added, "I jested with you, but the truth is, I really *do* only have my beauty to recommend me now. Papa does not forgive, and certainly not after discovering I quite literally jilted the Marquess of Pickering at the altar to follow Freddy on a madcap and ultimately failed elopement to Scotland."

Bracing for judgment, she raised her chin to look at Graeme.

"And now you know the sordid scandal and why I came to Shropshire."

Graeme watched her with a gaze so steady, so compassionate, she nearly broke. "Phoebe," he said softly, bringing her hand to his lips. "You are not ruined."

She looked away.

"I mean it." He brushed his lips against her knuckles, feather-light. "What that man did says everything about *him*. Nothing about you."

Her vision blurred, but she held fiercely to her composure.

"Thank you for trusting me," he added. "I am honored."

In a struggle to find her voice, she whispered, "I don't know why I told you."

"I do," he murmured.

She blinked up at him, rapidly trying to dispel the onset of tears over his kindness.

"Because you have a brave heart," he continued. "And because someone needed to tell you the truth of yourself. You deserve far more than you were given."

She bit her lip. Her heart was unfolding too quickly, too openly, and it frightened her.

"To ease the weight, I have a confession of my own." His gaze turned back to the easels, his thoughts miles away. "When my sister was around eight," he began, his tone heavy, "she attempted to teach me to paint the neighbor's cat. I produced an unfortunate creature, perhaps best resembling an elderly mole. To spare the household the anguish, we buried the sketch in the garden. To this day, neither of us has spoken of the tragedy."

Phoebe laughed. It was a tiny, watery laugh, but it was real and could not be helped. Graeme looked back at her with such gravity, she laughed harder still until her side hurt.

"So, you see," he said, "I understand that harsh feeling of failure."

"And you understand sisters," she added, quite meaning *women*, but she knew by his compassionate eyes, he understood precisely what she meant.

"And sisters," he agreed.

They tidied the brushes together, their hands touching frequently, each contact sending a frisson of heat through Phoebe. When she finally turned to leave, she hesitated, wishing to linger a while longer.

As did he.

"Until tomorrow?" he asked, voice low.

One breath.

Then two.

"Until tomorrow," she promised.

He reached as though to retake her hand, but stopped himself, and she nearly leaned forward to clasp his, but recovered. Their eyes met, a question left hanging, a longing left unspoken.

At last, she stepped back.

As she turned to leave, she felt his eyes on her, watching her follow the garden path back to the manor, his gaze warmer than the sunlight in her hair. When she glanced over her shoulder, just once, he was still watching her.

Still waiting.

Still hers.

Though neither dared name the feeling.

Chapter 15

Rain pearls clung to the windowpanes when Graeme arrived at the study after breakfast, the remnants of dawn's shower fading into pale streaks of sun. He had barely settled behind the desk when the butler entered with his usual martial efficiency and deposited a silver tray before him.

"Post, sir."

On the tray sat a single letter.

Thick parchment. Wax seal of deep green, a coronet pressed sharply into the center.

Graeme's pulse thudded.

The Marquess of Pickering.

For a moment, he simply stared, hands unmoving, as a tug of apprehension—nay, *hope*—tightened in his chest. His reckless letter of inquiry, sent in a moment of panic after receiving the estate solicitor's reply about Miss Whittington, had returned an answer. The pricey parchment chafed, a reminder of his initial distrust, of his hasty use of the Collumby seal, of how unnecessary all of it now felt. He trusted Phoebe implicitly; he needed no validation from a stranger.

And yet...

He broke the wax; curiosity piqued.

The marquess' handwriting was bold and uncompromising.

My Lord,

I have received your communication dated the 29ᵗʰ instant and make haste to answer it.

To your question: The Marchioness of Pickering does not bear the Christian name of Phoebe Whittington, rather J'non Gaines née Butler. The Marchioness, who is personally acquainted with the young lady of enquiry, speaks highly of her conduct and with consistent regard, &c. She is a young woman of admirable character and deserving of respect. Miss Whittington possesses both grace and integrity. I remain, my Lord, &c.

Pickering

Below this, in a sharper, more impatient scrawl were a few additional lines, unnecessary but unmistakably sincere, beginning with:

P.S. The Marchioness bids me add that she has always found Miss Whittington a young lady of excellent temper and admirable discretion.

And then followed with an additional postscript praise in the marchioness' neat hand, offering affectionate references, notes of resiliency, kindness, and loyalty. The final line of the letter, still in the marchioness' hand, read:

*A lady who holds her friends in genuine esteem
and is held in esteem by them.*

Graeme exhaled a long, unsteady breath. Then he
read the letter again. And again.

Not because he doubted its contents, but because
the words reshaped — no, *reaffirmed* — the perception
he had formed of her on his own.

Phoebe had told the truth. *About everything.* Not
one inconsistency had there been in her story, not
one manipulation. Even yesterday, especially yesterday, she had trusted him enough to confess what
must have cost her dearly, sharing her humiliation,
her heartbreak, her fears, and all the while he had
quietly harbored remnants of suspicion. He felt the
prick of guilt, subtle but undeniable.

Stronger than guilt was the swell in his chest of
something light and terrifyingly hopeful.

She was not ruined.

She was not disgraced.

She was not the desperate schemer he had once
foolishly, stupidly imagined.

She was... *Phoebe.* Entirely herself, candid,
sharp-witted, warm-hearted, and breathtak-
ingly brave.

Graeme folded the letter with care, as though it
were something fragile. His thumb brushed the seal
absently. A ridiculous urge overtook him: go to her at
once, tell her he believed her, apologize for ever doubt-
ing her, see the look she would give him when he told
her the marquess himself had praised her character.

No, wait. He wished to do these things, but he did
not desire for her to think he had snooped behind her

back or — *hush, Graeme. Only honesty will do. She is too perceptive for sidesteps.*

Truth be told, he wished to see her smile, wished to see her.

He rose before he realized he had stirred. The study felt suddenly too small for the feelings crowding him, the morning too long, the house too large of a distance between them.

Letter in hand, heart unmoored, he was determined to find Phoebe, and God help him, he doubted he could keep from touching her hand the moment he did.

The antechamber was as quiet as a chapel when Graeme emerged from the study, the marquess' letter warm in his hand, his heart warmer still. He hardly remembered the walk from desk to doorway. He only knew he had to find her.

Phoebe told the truth. She trusted me.

He passed the window overlooking the gardens and searched the parterres. Empty. It was one thing to want to see her and quite another to know where to begin his search. If not the gardens, where? The old library? He pivoted to the great doors. Poking his head in, he peered around and listened. Dim, still, untenanted. He reached the minstrel hall and paused, running a hand through his hair in restless thought. This early in the morning, she may still be breaking her fast or enjoying a leisurely morning toilette, out of his reach for another hour yet. He tugged at the tips of his hair.

A whim…

He took the stairs two at a time, his destination the portrait gallery. At the landing, he stopped to listen. A subtle echo of movement. Footsteps, light and unhurried, trailing down the long wing. He followed the sound. The door between the minstrel gallery and the portrait gallery stood ajar, morning sun pooling. He stepped inside.

Phoebe stood halfway down the long expanse, her back to him, the faint glow of light gilding the edges of her hair. She studied a grand ancestral portrait—one of the more forbidding Collumbys, jaw set like carved stone, martial expression as sharp as a sword—tilting her head in a way that made her curls sway. So arrested, he stood still. She looked utterly at home among the portraits of people she had never met.

He cleared his throat.

She turned.

Something inside his chest rearranged itself as the filtered light caught her expression, caught the *delight* at the sight of him.

"Mr. Ellison," she said, then corrected, "Graeme."

"Phoebe," was all he could manage.

In long strides, he closed the distance, slowing before her, not too near, not too far. The air between them sparked with some delicate and unnamable tension.

"I hope I'm not disturbing you," he said, though hope had nothing to do with it. He wanted to disturb her. Needed to. Was drawn to her as though every painted ancestor on the walls had conspired to usher him forward.

"You could never be a disturbance," she teased.

He swallowed, then, "I received a letter."

"Oh?" Her brows rose, curious and wary all at once, as though to say, *not again*.

Unperturbed by the eyebrows, he held out the letter. Tentatively, she accepted it, her fingers brushing his, leaving behind a warmth that lingered long after contact broke.

Flipping over the missive, she first noticed the broken seal, and then, "It's addressed to the Earl of Collumby."

He winced with a helpless shrug. "Yes. I'm afraid I… opened it," he admitted, defiant, embarrassed.

One corner of her mouth lifted. "A habitual opener of a peer's private correspondence?"

"Guilty."

"Bold." Her tone carried amusement, not censure.

Unfolding with a crackle of the wax, the edges crumpled from his having held it too close, too tight, she read it silently. The longer she scanned the page, the sharper his breath came, her only reveal a slight parting of lips. He watched her take in every word: the marquess' brisk praise, the marchioness' affectionate postscript, the final message written in a woman's thoughtful hand: *A lady held in genuine esteem by those who know her*. Or whatever had been the wording. He could not recall exactly.

When her eyes sought his, he was startled by their brightness. They glistened, but not with tears, rather relief, recognition, vindication. The letter crinkled when she lowered it.

"Graeme…" she said hoarsely.

His name in her voice unmade him utterly. "You are not ruined, not in the least. Not to anyone who matters."

Her lashes swept upward, catching the morning light. "You believe this?"

"I believe you." His voice thickened.

She exhaled, a light, breakable sound, half-laugh, half-breath of astonishment.

Without meaning to and without thinking to stop, he stepped closer.

She stepped towards him.

Letter clutched, her hand dropped to her side, as though weighed with everything she did not know how to say.

"Graeme…" she began anew, her voice trailing once more into silence.

Something unguarded flickered across her face. Hope? Fear? Longing? He could not be sure. He reached for her free hand, tentatively, reverently, giving her long moments to retreat. She did not. And then her fingers entwined with his. His heart tripped.

"Phoebe," he murmured, leaning until he felt her shaky breath against his cheek. "May I?"

The question, so simple, shivered between them.

Her hand tightened around his.

She nodded. Her lips parted, and in barely more than an exhale: "Yes."

He leaned closer, careful and gentle, as if the smallest haste might break the spell.

His lips brushed hers, feather-light, hesitant, trembling. She inhaled sharply.

He kissed her again. This time, deeper, still gentle, still cautious. His hand rose to cup the curve of her face, thumb skimming the silk of her cheek. In answer, she leaned into his palm. Her hand, letter forgotten, curled onto his sleeve, anchoring them, deepening the kiss further.

When they parted, neither breathed for a moment.

Her eyes fluttered open, dazed, shimmering. "Oh," she whispered.

He smiled, helpless, shaken, and in awe. "Oh, indeed."

They stood like that, suspended in the hush of the gallery, beneath the gaze of a hundred painted ancestors, all witnesses, no longer strangers.

At last, Phoebe stepped back, serene, as though floating on a dream. "I should…" she began, then faltered, cheeks pink.

"So should I," he echoed.

Neither moved.

Then, finally, she dipped her head, a secret smile tugging at her lips, and turned towards the minstrel gallery. She walked several steps before pausing to glance back. He watched her, too dazed to move, too captivated to do ought but smile. She broadened her returning smile, then disappeared around the corner, taking with her the marquess' letter.

Graeme touched his lips with a sigh.

For the first time since arriving at Lobelia Hall, he felt unmistakably alive *and entirely hers*.

Chapter 16

Graeme had never been more aware of his own heartbeat.

He stared down at the untouched cup of chocolate cooling on the desk, then at the doorway, then back at the cup, hoping the answer could be found within the dark depths—*how was a man supposed to behave the morning after kissing a woman who made the world tilt on its axis?*

He had barely slept. Every time he closed his eyes, he tasted sunlight and the miracle of her *yes*. And now, he had no earthly idea how to look her in the eyes.

A gentle knock broke through his thoughts. He nearly upset the chocolate.

"Mr... Graeme?" came the soft voice, *her* voice.

His pulse somersaulted.

The door cracked open, and Phoebe stepped inside, pausing in the doorway. Hands clasped before her, cheeks tinged with rose, and a shy smile told him she was as undone as he. But oh, that luminous smile... the world held its breath.

"Good morning," she said.

His reply stuck in his throat. "Good... good morning."

Brilliant, Graeme. Very suave.

Tucking a curl behind her ear, she looked everywhere except at him, the bookshelves, the windows, the tea tray, until at last, with effort, her gaze rose to meet his.

"Did you… sleep well?" she asked, then winced at her own question, painfully aware of its intimacy… or did she wince at his startled expression to have been asked so intimate a question?

"No," he blurted, then, in a panic, lest she misinterpret, "That is, I slept adequately. Perfectly adequately."

Silence followed. Not cold, not strained, *charged*, too full of yesterday morning to navigate. He should never have let her leave the gallery, not without something to anchor them to the day ahead. Another painting session, a walk, *anything*.

He gestured towards the tray in a hurried attempt at normality. "Would you care for chocolate? Or tea? I can ring…" *Good Lord, Graeme, stop talking.* "Tea?"

She tittered nervously. "Tea would be lovely."

He poured with unsteady hands. She reached to take the saucer at the same moment he passed it. Their hands bumped, fingers brushing.

She jerked away, startled.

He froze.

Her hand inched back towards the cup, fluttering with indecision. It struck him like a blow. Heat rose up his neck.

"Forgive me," he murmured. "I didn't mean—"

"No! No, it was only, I—" She fumbled. "I'm not usually so fidgety in the morning."

Breathe, man. She is embarrassed, not recoiling.

He covered his awkwardness with a smile. "Nor I."

Phoebe returned the smile, hers flickering between tender and timid, smothered beneath some delicate restraint neither seemed able to shake. Tea in hand, at last, she wandered towards a window and gazed out over the grounds.

"It's a lovely day," she said.

"Yes, it is."

Another hush. Comfortable, yet perilous, like standing at the edge of a cliff, the sea churning below.

She angled enough for him to see her profile in the morning light. Her lashes lowered. "About... yesterday."

His heart punched his ribs. "Yes?"

Was it his imagination, or did her fingers tighten around the teacup? "I hope I did not... behave foolishly."

Foolishly? *Foolishly? My Lord, had the moment meant so little to her?*

"No, you could never." He rose and approached her, but not close enough to touch. Oh, how he wanted to reach out, wrap an arm around her waist, pull her to him....

Her breath hitched, a small, telling sound, and she nodded but did not lift her gaze. And he did not reach for her.

How was he to read this moment? Or was it yesterday's moment that he had misread?

Returning her cup to the tray, she smoothed her hands over her gown. "I... I should go. I promised Fanny I would..."

"Of course," he said before she could finish, although every fiber within him wished to cry, "*Stay!*"

She moved towards the door with slow, uncertain steps. Reluctant to leave? At the threshold, she looked back, offering a meek smile that weakened his knees.

"Until later?" she asked.

"Yes. Later," he vowed.

And then she hurried away.

Graeme pressed his palms to the edge of the desk, grounding himself in the solid wood. Had he frightened her? Moved too quickly? Made himself too vulnerable with his earnest attraction? She did not *regret* the moment; he did not believe, but he wagered she was frightened. As was he. Not of the kiss, of everything it implied. *Only everything*.

With a sigh, he let his head fall forward. If he was not careful, if he kept tumbling towards her at this rate, he was going to lose his heart entirely. In fact, he suspected he already had.

Long after Phoebe's footsteps faded down the corridor, Graeme remained in the study, alone with the humming quiet she left behind. The silence felt different this morning, too sharp, too full, as though it carried the echo of her *yes* and the breathless press of her lips.

He had kissed her.

More impossible still: *she had kissed him back.*

He closed his eyes, letting the memory wash over him, recalling the tremble of her breath, the way her hand had curled onto his sleeve, the quiet little sound she made when he deepened the kiss. Heaven help him. He wanted her. Not in the idle, daydream way a man might admire a beautiful woman, but deep in his marrow, within the vulnerable place he had kept locked from the world. This wanting made everything inside him turn precarious.

And now, he replayed every detail of their parting. Her startled flinch when their hands touched, her shy question of how he slept, the nervous smile in the doorway. Embarrassment? Or regret? Had she enjoyed the moment in the gallery, or had she only submitted to the heat of that moment? She had teased him about being "a fellow tradesman," more truth than jest, perhaps. What future could she imagine with a humble clerk? What did she believe he could promise her? Love alone?

Graeme paced the room, dragging a hand through his hair. His steps, almost of their own volition, carried him to the locked drawer where the codicil lay hidden. His hand hovered over the brass handle. He knew every line of that cursed document by heart.

The inheritance would free her. Not only from her father but from the shadow of a ruined reputation and the necessity of marriage, free her from needing any man. It would free her to choose her own life.

Free her... from *him*.

The thought struck sharply, venomously. He braced himself against the desk, exhaling through the ache that if she learned of the codicil now, too soon, before there was anything solid between them, she would have no reason to stay. Independence would open every door she had been denied, and she would be free to choose any life she wished.

Why would she choose a life tied to him?

And yet… *he wanted her to have everything*.

He wanted her free and happy.

But he also wanted, God forgive him, *time*.

The moment he gave her the codicil, he would lose any hope of being counted among her choices. "She deserves freedom," he murmured to the empty room. "I *want* her to have the freedom she desires. But… I also want time…"

Time to know her.

Time to court her.

Time to see whether these feelings, wild, impossible, and glorious, could become something enduring.

Was it selfish to want this? Perhaps. Dishonorable to delay the codicil a little longer? Perhaps. But he was not denying her the inheritance forever, he reasoned, only borrowing a little time and courage before he handed her the freedom that might take her from him. At the back of his thoughts was the estate solicitor's most recent inquiry about the codicil, a brief and impatient letter from London, concerned only with the estate's precarious financial position and indifferent to the human cost of haste. Haste… the very element he did not want, not now.

He paced anew, mind racing ahead of his feet.

What if what they shared in the gallery was not merely a moment but the start of something *more*? What if she felt even a fraction of the pull he felt? What if he could show her that he was worthy of her trust? Worthier than her father, worthier than Freddy? What if she chose him *even after* she was free?

His breath caught.

Dangerous hopes. Foolish hopes. Hope, after all, was the most treacherous emotion of all.

Graeme sank into the chair, bracing his elbows on his knees and covering his face with both hands. He was not prepared for this. He certainly was not prepared for her, not for wanting her so fiercely so soon, or losing her before he had a chance.

Phoebe closed her chamber door with her back pressed against it, her breath catching in her throat as though she had run the length of the manor. She had expected to feel timid after the kiss, a little flustered, but never like *this*. This strange, uncontainable flutter beneath her ribs, a fire within her breast, spreading as if something in her had been cracked open and filled with light.

She pressed her fingers to her lips. They still tingled.

Graeme's kiss had not been stolen, not coaxed, not claimed. It had been gentle, devoted, intentional, a kiss that said *you matter*. No one had ever kissed her like that.

She crossed to the dressing table and sat, staring at but not seeing the painted chinoiserie. Then the humiliation of the morning returned in vivid detail: the way she had fumbled the teacup, stammered, asked that utterly dreadful question about whether he had slept. Saints preserve her. What sort of woman asked a man *that*?

But he had been so *formal*, so stiff, so unlike the man who had kissed her in the gallery. She had panicked. Surely he had regretted the kiss. Surely he feared she expected something from him now, courtship, promises, all the inevitabilities that followed a kiss.

But then… *did she* expect those things? No… but she hoped. Hope was a fragile creature, flightless but fluttering.

Love.

She had only just sworn it off, vowed she would never fall prey to such foolishness again. One kiss, and here she was, thinking of him, wanting him, aching from it all. But this was different. This was not gullibility falling for a practiced charmer. Graeme was no Freddy. He was… he was *genuine.*

And worst, most wonderful of all—

"He sees me," she whispered to the empty room.

He did not see her as her father's ornament, not a foolish girl who ruined herself on the promise of love, and especially not a dowryless burden.

No… he sees me.

The thought unraveled her.

Unsteady and terrifying, hope fluttered.

With trembling fingers, she traced the edge of the table.

Wanting was dangerous. Wanting had cost her everything once before. But… Graeme listened. Graeme cared. Graeme looked at her as though she were more than beauty and more than money.

Could he *truly* want her without money, though? A fine thing to *like* her, but could a trades-man-turned-solicitor, however kind, however good, afford to marry a woman who brought nothing with her but a tarnished name and a bruised heart? She had no dowry, no security, no father's approval, nothing to offer him, nothing to tempt him, nothing but herself. She knew all too well *she* was not enough.

She inhaled a shaky breath, gripping the table corner until the wood bit into her palm.

What if leaning into this, whatever this was, only made the fall harder? What if his awkwardness this morning had been a warning, and she was too giddy to heed that warning? What if he woke tomorrow and realized he wanted something simpler, cleaner, safer than a woman with her past?

Her heart twisted.

How humiliating it would be to want him more than he wanted her. How painful to reach out and find no hand reaching back.

Clutching her gown with her free hand, she swallowed against the sting behind her eyes. *Foolish, foolish girl! All this turmoil over one kiss and one awkward morning!*

Phoebe hardly knew herself now. The old Phoebe would have marched into the study, grabbed the man by his cravat, and kissed him senseless. But she was no longer that Phoebe. That girl had been cracked open and emptied. What remained was the fragile core of someone who had once believed in love, someone afraid to believe again.

This... this feeling for Graeme frightened her. It unsteadied her. It awakened something in her she thought long dead. She could not trust herself not to love him too much. Her heart beat too fast. Her fears tangled with yearning.

He had not yet claimed her heart, but his kiss had been enough to stir it from sleep.

Chapter 17

By early afternoon, sunlight streaked across the garden, turning each petal's glaze from the late morning's drizzle into a sparkling reflection. The study walls had begun to feel too narrow for the restless way his thoughts kept circling. Graeme stepped out onto the terrace in search of fresh air.

He lied.

He wanted to see her.

He had spent the morning pacing between desk, windows, door, and back again, thinking of her smile, the brush of her lips, the shy way she could not look at him in the study earlier that morning. Every light hesitation lodged inside him, knotting and tightening. *Does she regret it? Did I misread the moment? Did I go too far?*

As his gaze swept the garden, he told himself he was not *looking* for her, only steadying his breath.

It was ridiculous how much he needed the smallest reassurance of mutual attraction. But this was not a mild infatuation, or at least he did not want it to be, not with Phoebe.

Crossing into the gardens, he followed the first path. Only minutes had passed since he had spied her from the study window, meandering through parterres. Down another path, he wandered. Since that morning, he had thought about what to do, how much to say, how much to wait, how to place the truth in her hands without losing her.

Halfway down the slope, he spotted her.

His pulse thumped.

She stood near the fountain, fingertips grazing the cool spray, the hem of her gown catching the faint breeze. Her curls, styled loosely, caught the sun, turning raven tresses to honeyed silk. She did not hear him approach. For a moment, he simply watched her, admiring how achingly lovely she looked, feeling the familiar shift in his chest. Something inside him reached for her.

Before he could talk himself out of it, allowing doubts and fears to win, he walked towards her. "Phoebe," he said softly, not wanting to startle her.

Phoebe turned, startled anyway, but then, upon seeing him, her lips curved into a deep, genuine smile with only hints of shyness. "Graeme."

"May I join you?" he asked.

"Yes, yes, of course."

They fell into step beside one another, neither immediately speaking, the air between them charged with anticipation.

"I hope you're well?" he ventured.

She nodded. "Perfectly. And you?"

"Perfectly," he echoed, though his heartbeat contradicted him with every thrum.

They reached the linden tree, the ground beneath dappled with sunlight. Graeme searched for the words to break this infernal awkwardness. Perhaps he had pushed too much too fast. After all she had been through, she may need more time, a slower pace.

Phoebe plucked the branches overhead, tittering over the sprinkle of droplets they sprayed. "I keep thinking about our painting." Her tone was light, but there was something almost fragile beneath, something that had his pulse quickening, tripping, and misbehaving entirely. Teasing, she said, "I still cannot believe you let me produce such a catastrophe in your company. You are either the most noble man I've ever met or a seasoned fibber."

"Your artistry held no end to charm. I shall treasure the watercolor always. In fact, I intend to frame it, complete with a placard that reads, 'brave hedgehog-leaf attempting to climb tree.'"

Her eyes widened in indignation before she dissolved into laughter. "I never stood a chance," she said. "How you managed to keep a straight face I'll never know."

"I thought only of your bravery to allow your foxed squirrel loose on the page."

She elbowed him in the ribs. "You are impossible!"

Wincing playfully, he absorbed her touch greedily.

Tugging her bottom lip between her teeth, she met his gaze, then looked away. "These have been the happiest days I've had in a long time…"

His heart thumped wildly.

She stared back at the garden rather than at him, as if afraid of her own honesty, or perhaps his reaction.

He stepped closer, not touching, but close enough to hear her sharp intake of breath. "For me, as well."

Finally, she lifted her gaze, her eyes meeting his, uncertain and hopeful. "Truly?"

"Truly."

A delicate silence enfolded them, a silence that said *I want more.* Could she feel it as strongly as he could?

His hand lifted slightly, then stilled, the desire to caress her cheek painfully strong, but the thought was too tender a risk. Instead, he cleared his throat. "There is something I should tell you."

Her posture tensed. "Something... troubling?"

"Only news that will change the household, news that arrived late this morning." Then, reassuring, he added, "Nothing troubling. Only, I want you to be the first to know."

Turning fully towards him, expression tight with unease, she echoed, "News?"

"The Earl of Collumby is expected at Lobelia Hall."

She exhaled a surprised "Oh."

That single sound — *oh* — held something he could not pinpoint, something weighty, but it was neither dread nor relief.

"Soon?"

"I've not an exact date," he fibbed, "but soon enough that preparations must begin."

She looked back to the manor, brows knitting. "Everything will change when he arrives."

Graeme's chest tightened. "Not everything."

Worrying her lips, she turned back to him. "Won't it?"

"Not... unless you want... change."

For a moment, she searched his face, but he could not say what she sought. Then, she stepped closer, close enough for him to feel her warmth, close enough that only a single handspan separated them.

Voice lowered, she said, "Our time together... *yesterday*... it means something to me. Only... tell me now if I've imagined it meaning... *more*."

He swallowed. "Oh, Phoebe. If you've imagined it, then we're sharing the same fantasy."

A trembling smile broke across her lips. "If things do change with his arrival, I need you to know I don't want to lose... this... with you. I *want* this... and more."

Hoarsely, his pulse thundering, he said, "Then, we are of one mind."

Before he could gather breath or thought, Phoebe reached for him, not boldly or brazenly, but with shaky courage, slipping her hand into his and lacing their fingers. The warmth between them felt achingly familiar. Yesterday's whispered *yes* echoed through him. Stepping onto her toes, she pressed a feather-light kiss to his cheek, just at the corner of his mouth, soft enough to sear him to the bone.

A promise.

A reassurance.

A quiet *I want you too*.

When she drew back, her cheeks were flushed and her eyes shining. "Fanny will wonder where I've vanished to." Her words whispered with smiling breathlessness.

Graeme clung to her hand for a last heartbeat, his chest aching to keep her by his side. "Phoebe, I—"

"It'll keep until later," she said, glowing with hope. "Yes?"

"Yes, it'll keep."

She stepped away slowly, lightly tugging at his hand, their fingertips sliding inch by blessed inch, lingering between them before she released him, then turned back towards the manor. Only when she reached the bend in the path did she glance back with one luminous, devastating smile before she disappeared into the sunlit corridor of hedges.

Graeme pressed a hand to his chest.

God help him. He would give her the world if she asked for it.

Chapter 18

The setting sun pooled long streaks across the antechamber, deceptive in their implied warmth. The walls were cold to the touch. Phoebe stood before the study door, smoothing a hand over her gown with a fluttery exhale she could neither control nor hide, not even from herself. She had not meant to come here. Truly, she had not. In her defense, it was not after dark this time, but that did not make this visit any more proper.

She had gone up to her chamber after the garden walk, intending to read or sew or do some other lady-like and sensible activity befitting a woman who had just admitted that she wanted *more* from a man, an admission that did not mean she admired or idly fancied him, rather wanted him, heart-first and help-lessly. It was too soon to call this love, too soon to think the word *marriage*, but she did want that some-thing more that would determine if those could be on the horizon, if this could be something enduring. She wanted it to be. Oh, how she wanted it to be.

Heart full, she had reached for paper instead of an embroidery hoop. She had written a few hesitant words, intended to be confessions of her heart. But she ripped up the note almost immediately. Then tried again. And again.

The letter — that foolish, hopeful letter — now held folded in her hand, pressed against her palm. She had no intention of giving it to him directly; good heavens, she was not that brave. But she could leave it on his desk, quietly and discreetly. A note of fondness, of... *possibility*.

Heart thudding, she knocked lightly and waited. No answer.

"Graeme?" She opened the door a sliver.

Silence.

He was not there. Relief and disappointment tangled as she stepped into the room. The late afternoon light poured through the tall windows, casting a haze. His teacup still sat on the tray, a book facedown on the settee; he had only stepped out for a moment, then. She swallowed, nerves alive and skittering.

Leave the note.

Do not linger.

Do not, dear heaven, overthink.

She approached the desk. His chair was slightly askew, as though he had risen in haste. Papers lay in gentle disarray, a ledger half-open, the blotter pushed to one side. Something about the sight made her smile: he had been restless, too, after the garden tryst. Was he thinking about the same *possibilities* as she? Or was he concerned over the earl's impending arrival, fretting over preparations and, possibly, wondering how to rationalize his romance with a woman who had been a guest of the house?

Clutching her note, she reached for an empty corner near the blotter where she might set it in bold view, unmistakably propped when he returned. She leaned it against the blotter, just so. Hmm. Perhaps it needed —

— a single sheet, half covered by the ledger, caught the faintest movement when she nudged her note.

A curved flourish at the top… and…

Miss P.W.

Another letter from the earl, then. She never wanted to see those dreadful letters again. But her eyes had already betrayed her, darting across the page, snagging on phrases before she even knew she was reading.

This was *not* another letter.

This was a bequest.

Looking around her to ensure she remained alone, she angled the page just enough.

Provision for Miss P.W… unentailed wealth in the sum of approximately thirty thousand pounds… to be transferred upon presentation… my dearest companion of spirit… ensure she is cared for… a small cottage…

Phoebe's stomach hollowed as she continued to scan the page, unable to stop.

I think only of your happiness… You deserve more than life has given you… I can leave you assurance…

Her hand flew to her mouth. No. No, this could not be real, could not be for her, could not —

But who else? Who else in Lobelia Hall carried P.W. as her initials? Who else fit the situation and inexplicable tenderness of the late earl's journal entries? Her knees weakened. She sank into the chair. In her ears, her pulse roared. This was not some whimsical affection or pleasant correspondence. This was a legally binding promise, as well as a fortune.

But why?

The earl had never met her. She had never written to him. Had Papa misled him, convinced of something never offered, that she was more than she was? Oh, how tragic that a dying man had believed she would come to him any minute and be at his bedside, that although he contracted the marriage in hopes of begetting an heir, he had died with delusions of love, died expecting her to come to him before his last breath, the sunshine of his declining years.

Shame and guilt gripped her throat.

No, no, no, this could *not* refer to her, despite that Fanny had believed unquestioningly the initials on the letters had been hers, despite that even Graeme had believed the initials in the journal—*Graeme*.

Her breathing sharpened. She gasped violently.

Graeme had known.

Graeme had known before the journal, before the letters, of Miss P.W.

Graeme had known there was a bequest waiting for her, one that would tip the fates.

He had known all along.

And *he had never told her.*

Her pulse pounded in her ears, reverberating through her skull.

His kiss, his tenderness, the gentle way he said her name, all the ways he made her feel seen, valued, wanted — Good Lord above, she had been nothing but a purse to him.

Then she saw it all, clear as a summer day. Just like Freddy's false sweetness, his devotion when her dowry had seemed secure, and then his abandonment when the dowry was lost. Her vision blurred, and her throat burned.

Tucking the codicil where she found it, she smoothed the ledger over top, so the paper lay exactly, precisely as before. She would not allow him to know she had seen it. She would not give him the satisfaction of witnessing her humiliation. Oh, to think she had even confessed her gullibility to him when she told him about Freddy! How he must have laughed at her!

It was all about money. It was always about money. Papa was right.

Phoebe snatched her letter, the hopeful confession of adoration, folded it into a tiny square, all while swiping at her water-brimmed eyes, and tucked it into her stays to dispose of elsewhere. What a time to be without a pocket or reticule! Of one thing she was certain, he would never read her honeyed words. Not now. Not ever. What a lark he would have to see how easily she had been swayed. All her protests, yet she had walked right into his trap. A few whispered words, and she had been convinced this was real, ready to jaunt yet again to the altar in the belief of true love, all so a greedy and penniless man could realize wealth.

Her heart hammered painfully as she forced herself to stand, gripping the edge of the desk, willing her strength to return so she could leave with dignity. Heaven forbid any of the servants see her so undone. Her eyes burned, but she refused to cry here. Oh, she hated this room! He had embraced her like she mattered, all while knowing she was to be his inheritance, the quickest and easiest money earned, no need to slave for an earl as a man of business with such a sum.

She turned towards the door. Escape was her only option. She must leave before he returned. He must never know she had been there.

Graeme headed for the study, pulse thrumming an eager, boyish rhythm. Since their moment in the garden, since her quiet admission of wanting *more*, he had been unable to think of anything except seeing her again. So restless, he had roamed the hall in hopes of bumping into her, rehearsing a dozen pretty speeches on his ramble. None felt adequate, but he was quite determined to set everything into motion.

Hand on the latch, he stepped inside.

Phoebe barreled into him, sending him stumbling against the doorframe. With a sharp inhale, he clasped her arm to keep her from tripping over him, she looking as startled as he.

When her gaze met his, he felt a queer tug in his chest he could not explain. Her eyes did not brighten as they had in the garden when he approached her, rather they... no, he could not put it into words. Something distant, something contained. He was overthinking, of course. Nervous about confessing his growing affection.

Or perhaps she was embarrassed to be caught waiting for him? Yes, that must be it! Well, he would set her at ease. If only she knew he had been searching for her moments before!

"Phoebe," he said, filling the single word with all the tenderness he possessed.

She stepped away, bowing her head.

"I hadn't expected you would come here."

With a whisper of a smile, she murmured, "I hope you don't mind."

"Mind? Never." He held a hand towards the settee in invitation, every step measured so he would not seem overeager. "I was looking for you, actually."

"Were you?"

"Yes." He swallowed his fears, hoping to gather courage. "There is something I must tell you."

She gasped a little sound of surprise, a wistful sound that made his heart soar. Could she anticipate what he wished to say? Had she come here to confess similarly? When she did not accompany him to the settee, he considered this a hopeful reaction. After all, he was too restless to sit, as well. Best to stand. Yes, she had the right of it.

"I mean to be honest," he began, "and clear. These past few days, no, these past few weeks have... they have been among the happiest of my life."

She listened, her lashes tremoring slightly.

"I know you have every reason to be cautious, every reason to doubt the intentions of men. I don't want to press you, overwhelm you, or expect anything from you that you are not ready to give."

She continued to listen intently.

"I... I wish you to know... I... I care for you, sincerely, more than I intended, more than I thought possible, more than I ought this early in our friendship." He took a deep breath. "My affections for you run deeply, beyond physical attraction. You are the wittiest, cleverest, boldest woman I've had the privilege to know, and I... I want to court you, Phoebe. Properly. With your permission."

Her lips parted, as though to speak, but then her expression changed, a subtle tightness she hid behind a shy smile of uncertainty. Again, he felt that peculiar tug in his chest, but he could not understand it.

When she did not reply after a long stretch of silence, he asked, his heart in his throat, "Phoebe? Is something wrong?"

Too quickly, she answered, "No, oh, nothing is wrong. I only —" She looked down at her hands, clasping them together. "It's simply... very sudden."

Of course. His heart cinched. He had overwhelmed her despite his wish not to do just that. He had moved too fast and should have given them more time. After all she had been through...

"I understand," he said. "Truly. You needn't answer me now. We have all the time in the world."

"I appreciate that." Her fingers trembled. "This is a great deal to consider."

Consider. His hope wavered but did not extinguish. She had not rejected him or recoiled. Only... he had rather hoped, after the garden, she might be so overcome she would wrap her arms around his neck and... well.... This was not the reaction he had hoped, but it was the reaction he should have expected from a woman who had been so deeply wounded before.

"Of course. Take all the time you need," he said.

Flexing her fingers, then lacing them again, she took a step towards the door. "I should... go."

His pulse stuttered. "Phoebe —"

She offered a soft smile, polite and composed, painfully unlike the Phoebe who had kissed him beneath the linden tree hours earlier.

"Thank you for your honesty," she said with a slight bow of her head.

And then she was gone.

The door shut behind her soundlessly.

Graeme stood still, rooted, the air of the study shifting around him, sending a faint chill down his back. Slowly, he lowered himself into the desk chair, staring at the place where she had been standing moments ago. He had confessed his desire to court her. He had offered everything he dared. Instead of leaning towards him, she had withdrawn. Perhaps he was being foolish and asking too much too soon. She had not been angry or disgusted, anything that signified rejection. She had only needed time. And why not? He must have frightened her with the depth of his feelings, for she would know as well as he what courtship meant. No idle garden flirtation. Was it that Freddy's ghost still lingered between them?

He dragged a hand down his face. It could not be because she thought of him as a tradesman. It could not.

"She needs time," he said to the empty room with feigned confidence. "Of course I will give her time."

Every instinct urged him to race after her and pull her into his arms, but he would wait. He would be patient. He would show her with patience and consistency that this was not a passing fancy.

The hours crawled.

By the time the sun began its slow descent on the day following his courtship proposal, Graeme had replayed every breath of their conversations, from the kiss in the gallery to her request for time to consider. The words frayed.

He had not seen her since she left the study. Not in the corridors. Not in the garden. Not in the gallery. Either she was dodging him to bide more time, or she had sequestered herself in her chamber to avoid him. This did not bode well. Where had he gone wrong? Had she not encouraged him during their garden assignation, he would think he had misread her reactions and insulted her, but she *had* encouraged him. She had wanted *more*. Her words.

He had not eaten a full meal since she left the study. He had not done any work either. Listless, he wandered.

After the longest day of his life, Graeme found himself drifting towards the study, his feet carrying him without decision. The door yielded beneath his hand. The room was dim, washed in the pale lavender of dusk. If his heart thumped a little faster in hopes of spying a particular young lady waiting for him, he would admit it to no one, especially after finding the room empty. Not even the essence of orange blossoms lingered, as though she had never been there.

How different the air felt. Heavy. Stale.

He stopped halfway between the door and the desk, lost.

With the steward taking his place in the new study, and the estate solicitor soon to return to Lobelia Hall to resume his place in the old study, where was Graeme to reside? One of the libraries, perhaps. Or he could tell the estate solicitor or steward to move their desk. Now that he was thinking on it, with the earl's impending arrival, he should extend an invitation to his trade solicitor, Mr. Brant Ellison, although the man might prefer to stay in London to see to business matters—too many solicitors, he mused. For that matter, what was he to do with the family trade now that he decided to reside at Lobelia Hall permanently?

All these points he should have decided by now, but he had been too distracted by a certain bold woman with sooty lashes. Graeme sank into the desk chair and stared at the scattered papers, untouched since his encounter with Phoebe.

He stared, unseeing, his thoughts whirling.

He should write to his mother and sister. A letter was long overdue. They would need to know he had decided it was time for the earl's arrival.

He stared, unseeing.

Yes, he should write to them.

He sighed.

Paper. He needed paper to write a letter.

He stared.

Then he saw it. Peeking from beneath the top-most ledger was a corner of cream paper. His eyes widened. His breath sharpened. His heart thumped.

The codicil.

It was not revealed for all to see, tucked as it was under the ledger, but the hair on the back of his neck stood on end as a shiver snaked down his spine. He never left important papers unguarded. Not ever. Until now. A dull shock moved through him. He had been so consumed by thoughts of her, so rattled by her tenderness, that he had forgotten prudence altogether. *Fool! Careless fool! One moment's distraction, and I left the most dangerous paper in the estate lying half-exposed!*

Had she seen it?

He did not dare move, suspended between dread and disbelief, hands gripping the arms of the chair. Searching the desk, his eyes flicked this way and that. Not even the faintest sign of disturbance. Why would she have seen it? He tried to rationalize the situation. There would have been no reason for her to sit at the desk, no reason to sift through the papers. More pointedly, if she *had* seen it, she would not have withdrawn behind polite smiles, not Phoebe, rather she would have railed at him as soon as he walked into the room, scolded him for not telling her right away.

Shakily, he exhaled.

If she had seen it…

If she had read it…

His throat tightened.

She would know the late earl left her a fortune. She would also know Graeme had concealed it from her.

He pressed a hand to the back of his neck. The room blurred as panic swelled.

No, he reasoned once more. She would have said something. Phoebe would not hide indignation. She would not retreat to her chamber. She would confront him.

Would she not?

Massaging the back of his neck, he tried to think, tried to recall her exact words, exact reactions. The inability to meet his eyes, the reluctance to speak, the eagerness to be away from him… none of these gave the smallest reassurance, not from the woman who had said earlier that same day, "*Tell me now if I've imagined it meaning more.*"

If she had seen the codicil, she would know she did not need him or any man. She was free. She was free from her father, from Freddy's shadow, from marriage altogether. She could live as she pleased, independent, beholden to no one. What a temptation that must be for a woman who had been trapped her entire life, far and away more tempting than a tradesman's proposal for courtship.

What place did a humble clerk have in her heart when she was independently wealthy?

He *wanted* her to have freedom, to have her own life, her own choices, her own future. He *wanted* her to choose love with no expectations, no debts, no coercion. He wanted this above all things. But… he feared she had already chosen independence over love. And his hands were tied.

Need coursed through his veins, the need to go to her, to storm into her suite and plead she consider *him*. Would both fates not be ideal? Money *and* love? She could have both, he could argue.

No, no, he needed to give her time and space to make her own decision. She must choose freely if she wanted just the inheritance or if she would consider taking a chance on love, and this must be her decision fully. He had kept this from her long enough.

His gaze drifted towards the window where the last threads of daylight slipped behind the grove. Why bother preparing for the earl's arrival now when everything he hoped to build with Phoebe was uncertain? A chill in the air shivered through him. He could do nothing except wait. If she wished to speak with him, she would come. If she wished to choose him, she would come. If not... well... this was her choice to make, even if that choice broke his heart.

Chapter 19

When Mrs. Redshaw's voice floated beyond the study door around noon, the rain had settled into a fine, drifting mist.

"Mr. Ellison? There's a young woman here requesting an audience."

Graeme lifted his head from the half-written letter to his mother. The housekeeper's tone carried a tightness, what he interpreted as a combination of disapproval and embarrassment.

Tucking the quill into its stand, he pushed away from the desk and swallowed his wishful thinking that it was Phoebe wishing to see him. "Show her in."

Mrs. Redshaw opened the door but hesitated over the threshold before stepping aside to reveal a slight woman in a patched pelisse, a child perched on her hip. The boy clung to her like a barnacle, face buried in her shawl, though a mop of pale curls peeked out. If Graeme hazarded a guess, he would say the boy was around two years of age, but possibly older.

The woman dipped a curtsy, eyes lowered. "Beggin' your pardon, sir. Penelope Woodridge." Her voice was slightly worn at the edges, vowels pressed close but not rough, almost melodic, in a way.

"Please, come in."

Woodridge. The name was unfamiliar.

She crossed into the room with timid steps, sparing only a glance at Mrs. Redshaw's departure. The boy hid his face when Graeme tried to get a better look at him.

"No need to fear, lad," Graeme offered.

Mrs. Woodridge shifted her weight, patting the child's back. "He's a shy one, sir. Don't speak much to strangers."

Graeme motioned for her to sit.

She did not.

"Please, sit, Mrs. Woodridge."

"Miss. But beggin' your pardon, I prefer Penny." Another tiny curtsy, then she approached the chair as though it might bite.

She took so long to study the chair, her gaze sweeping anxiously around the room before returning with slight trepidation to the chair, that Graeme almost extended the invitation again. But at length, she perched on the edge, so far on the edge she might take flight at the slightest invitation, one hand smoothing the boy's hair either to quiet him or her own nerves.

"I understand you requested an audience."

"I'm hopin' to petition the new earl." She narrowed her gaze. "You him?"

Graeme cleared his throat. "I serve as his solicitor in his absence. You may speak freely."

Miss Woodridge swallowed, fingers twining in her son's hair. "Aye, sir, thank you. I... I'm hopin' for a character. A letter, like. Somethin' to say I weren't dismissed for bein'... wicked." Her gaze lowered.

"There's places will still hire on a girl if she's steady enough. But none'll take on a gel that's…" Her voice trailed off.

The boy curled closer.

"I understand." He nodded to the child. "You have a son."

Looking up at him, her eyes burned with mortification, but her chin held a tiny thread of pride. "Aye, sir. Nearly three, he is. Good boy. Quiet. Don't make trouble."

The boy peeked at Graeme with solemn blue eyes before hiding again.

Graeme wished Mrs. Redshaw had spoken with him privately before seeing Miss Woodridge to the study. He could not fathom what this was all about. "Tell me why you believe the earl might vouch for you."

She hesitated, then slowly drew a small cloth bundle from her pocket, a few papers wrapped in faded muslin. "He… he used to write me, sir. Said he didn't like to trouble the steward with nonsense, so he'd write me little notes, sayin' I'd done good work, or bringin' a bit o' advice." Her cheeks flushed. "Only… only I can't read, sir. Never learned. He'd read 'em aloud when I were in the room. Never let me keep 'em, but… I kept some. Thought maybe…" She bit her lip, pushing the letters towards Graeme with trembling hands. "That it might help show I weren't tossed out for bein' idle or impertinent."

Graeme unwrapped the cloth and sifted through the papers. His pulse thudded. The handwriting was unmistakably the late earl's slanted, sprawling script. For a moment, he had thought she was to claim the new earl had written to her, which would be quite impossible, but now he saw that was not the case after all.

He unfolded the first page and read it. Not a letter. Notes about grouse baiting. He flicked his gaze to her hopeful expression. Second paper... not a letter either, a list of port bottles suitable for the cellar. Third paper...

Graeme blinked.

A limerick. And a thoroughly indecent one at that. Heat crept up his neck. He folded it with decisive speed. Then his hands stilled.

For My Little P.W.

Graeme stared at the notation, eyes focusing and unfocusing.

Penelope Woodridge.

P.W.

When he looked up, he saw her watching him, a nervous tick to her brow.

"They're the only ones I could hide away, sir. I was sent off quick after... after he died. Mrs. Redshaw said it weren't fitting for me to stay. And I didn't argue none. I knew she were right. Only..." Her voice cracked. "Only, I ain't had steady work since. Not for weeks now. Soon as they learned I had a babe, they said there weren't a place for the likes of me. I don't need charity, sir, only a decent word put in."

A more naïve man might have missed the desperation under her controlled humility. Graeme had seen it too many times in London.

He leaned back, studying her with new insight. "Miss Woodridge—"

"Penny, if you please."

"…Penny… the late earl treated you kindly?"

She angled her head, her pinched brows showing puzzlement over the question. "Aye. At first, I were frightened of 'im. All them wigs and waistcoats, and his tempers, and the way he'd look at me sometimes…" Another faint flush. "But he were generous. Gave me trinkets, ribbons for my hair. Always said I had a pretty smile."

He knew where this was going before she continued. He saw it all too clearly. What he was unsure of was her position with the estate, or former position, rather, although it was clear enough she had been an employed servant of some sort, a maid, but he could not guess beyond that, be she a former parlor maid, scullery maid, or otherwise. Not that it mattered.

"'Tweren't love, sir. Don't think that. Only… kindness I didn't expect. And after the boy came, he kept me on. Didn't turn me out. I was grateful for that."

Graeme's eyes landed on the boy, his heart hammering. *Ah.* Even as the truth sat before him, the entirety had not yet dawned. He leaned forward.

The truth lay plainly. Not a romance. Not seduction from her side. A frightened girl indulging the whims of a lonely old man. Graeme exhaled slowly, trying to take it all in. *This boy was most likely the late earl's illegitimate son.*

Everything he had believed, everything he had feared, everything he had accused Phoebe of… all of it crumbled inside him.

"I will need to speak with Mrs. Redshaw," he said. "And with the clergyman who witnessed the cod—" He stopped himself. *Careful.* "—who handled some of the late earl's business," he finished instead.

Miss Woodridge clutched her son closer. "I've not caused trouble, sir. I swear it. I only want work. I'll scrub floors or wash linens or—"

"You will cause no trouble," Graeme said firmly. "You have done nothing wrong. You have been sinned against, not sinning."

She blinked a few times, either surprised by his words or combating emotions, he could not tell which.

"Return tomorrow afternoon," he said. "I will have answers for you then."

"Thank you, sir."

As she left the study, the child raised his head, eyes wide, and spoke a single shy word: "Bye." Then he hid again against his mother's shoulder.

Graeme stood still as the door clicked shut.

P.W.

Penelope Woodridge.

Not Phoebe. Never Phoebe.

He pressed a shaking hand to the desk. This changed both everything and nothing. Because Phoebe still had not chosen him. And he had no earthly idea how to mend the mess.

Graeme found Mrs. Redshaw in the stillroom, sleeves rolled, supervising jars of dried herbs and peppermint. She stiffened the moment she saw him, a slight, instinctive tightening around the eyes that told him she already sensed why he had come.

"Mrs. Redshaw," he said. "A word, if you please."

She folded her hands, composed as ever. "Of course, Mr. Ellison."

He gestured towards the nearby worktable. "Shall we?"

She perched on the bench with the dignity of a woman who had run households larger and more distinguished than Lobelia Hall. Graeme remained standing, not out of superiority, but because his thoughts would not allow him stillness.

"As you know, I spoke today with Penelope Woodridge."

The housekeeper's lips pursed, color rising in her cheeks. "A most improper young woman, sir. Her coming here, bold as you please, was almost more than I could credit."

"Improper," he echoed. "Because she has a child?"

Mrs. Redshaw straightened, bristling. "Because she was... *involved* with His Lordship."

Graeme watched her carefully. "And yet you never came forward with that information when the... when certain documents came to light. Your signature bears witness."

She stiffened. "I did not think it my place, sir. The chaplain was the other witness. I assumed he had spoken to the solicitor who attended His Lordship. It would have been most inappropriate for me to bring up such... sordid matters." Her chin lifted defensively. "A housekeeper does not discuss her master's *lapses* with strangers."

"Even when a woman's livelihood depended on it?"

Mrs. Redshaw faltered. "I dismissed her because it was needful. The household was in disarray after the master died. There was gossip among the maids, and I could not allow... impropriety to stain the new earl's first days. Better she start afresh elsewhere. I did advise her to seek a post outside Shropshire."

Inhaling deeply, Graeme said, "Which she attempted. And was dismissed repeatedly once her circumstances became known."

A sheen of guilt flickered in the older woman's eyes. "I did what I believed right for the house. The reputation of Lobelia Hall matters, sir. If it were known a maid, *my* maid, had allowed such familiarity with the master..." she stammered, "I... I feared the new earl might dismiss me, too."

Graeme's brows lifted with painful understanding.

Fear. Reputation. Assumptions. Pride.

How many lives had the late earl bent or broken out of selfish loneliness? How many people trembled still beneath the weight of his choices?

Graeme ran a thumb along the edge of the worktable. "You witnessed the document discussing Miss Woodridge's... provision."

Her voice dropped to barely a whisper. "Aye. The master insisted that the chaplain and I sign as witnesses. He seemed quite set on it. I thought it best forgotten afterward." She cast her eyes downward. "I did not realize the young woman had not been informed. Nor that it should fall to you to untangle."

"Mrs. Redshaw, I don't accuse you of malice. But secrecy, however well-intentioned, has consequences. Miss Woodridge and her son are in need. The new earl will honor the late earl's provisions."

She nodded once, hands folded tightly, relief loosening the lines of her face. "I am grateful, sir."

Graeme hesitated, then asked, "And Miss Whittington? Have you seen her these past two days?"

Mrs. Redshaw raised her eyebrows. "Miss Whittington? No, sir. I assumed she remained in her rooms. The weather has been poor for strolling. Shall I send word up to her, if you wish to speak with her?"

His heart tugged, an ache he was becoming far too accustomed to. "No, not yet. That won't be necessary."

She rose, adjusting her apron. "Will you require anything further, Mr. Ellison?"

"No, thank you."

She bobbed a nod and returned to supervising the herbs, though her hand shook faintly as she set a jar back on its shelf.

Graeme closed the stillroom door behind him with care.

Penelope Woodridge had told the truth, as he knew she had. Mrs. Redshaw confirmed it.

And Phoebe... Phoebe believed him a liar, or worse. He pressed a hand to his forehead. One more conversation, then he could set things right— with both Penelope Woodridge and the woman he loved.

The Lobelia Hall chaplain was exactly where Graeme expected him, polishing one of the brass candlesticks with the care of a man who believed cleanliness next to godliness was not a metaphor but a liturgical requirement.

"Mr. Ellison," said the chaplain, setting aside the candlestick. "I heard the new earl is due to arrive at last. I had begun to wonder if I should see you before then." He wiped his brow with a linen handkerchief. "Pray tell me this is not further calamity with the roof tiles. They have been hanging by the grace of God alone."

Graeme managed a smile. "The roof may rest safe another day. I've come about the late earl."

"Ah?" He straightened, curiosity wrinkling his forehead.

Stepping to the front pew, Graeme rested a hand on its edge. "Penelope Woodridge came to the Hall today."

"Is she well? I've been concerned. Her circumstances were… precarious."

"She has struggled more than we may know. I understand you witnessed the document in which the late earl indicated her financial provision."

Studying the candlestick with reverence, he said, "It surprised me at the time. The master's health was failing. I was called. Mrs. Redshaw was present. He requested prayer and witness of the codicil. I assumed the matter would pass directly to the estate solicitor."

Graeme pressed. "You never spoke to the solicitor?"

"I had no reason to. It was not my position to meddle in the legal affairs of the peerage. A clergyman keeps confidences. And as Miss Woodridge was shortly gone from the estate, I imagined the matter had been handled."

"Miss Woodridge never learned of the provision."

A pained look crossed the chaplain's face. "The poor girl. She is terribly young. Innocent, though life has not allowed her the luxury of innocence since." He folded his hands. "The earl treated her with a sort of fondness. I do not excuse him. It was an unbalanced attachment. He was powerful, while she was vulnerable, dependent."

Graeme considered the harm done by both the housekeeper's and the chaplain's silence, yet their reasoning made perfect sense, each assuming the other would confer with the solicitor, and each assuming the other had already done so, all taken care of with little bother to themselves. Then, had the estate solicitor known the identity of Miss P.W. from the outset, would ought have been different with his request of Graeme to see the beneficiary relinquish her inheritance or face them in court? Graeme doubted it. But at least there would not have been the confusion with Phoebe.

The chaplain sighed. "The earl was a man who lived and died by his pride. If you will permit me to say, I believe his affection for the girl was genuine, in his own way. He spoke to me often about his brother's disgrace, marrying beneath him, as he said. It consumed the man to think the family name might be mocked."

The weight of the lineage settled on Graeme's shoulders with its prejudices and its cruelties.

"Tell me, sir, does His Lordship intend to honor the codicil?"

"Yes, he will honor it."

Graeme closed his eyes briefly, Phoebe's face rising unbidden in his mind, bearing wounded betrayal of an inheritance never meant to be hers. How cruel of the earl, he thought, to leave nothing at all for her, knowing full well she was on her way to the Hall with expectations of marriage — a double betrayal, by Graeme's estimation.

"God be praised. It will change that girl's life. And, if you'll permit me to say, redeem a portion of the late earl's."

Graeme's throat tightened at the last. "Thank you. You've been helpful."

"If Miss Woodridge needs anything, you may send her to me. And if *you* need counsel, Mr. Ellison, my door is always open."

Nodding gratefully, Graeme left the chaplain to his candlesticks.

Chapter 20

Morning found Graeme pacing, Phoebe's absence shadowing every breath. He had not slept. But duty demanded action, and Penelope Woodridge was due within the hour.

So distracted, he did not hear the knock. He stood near the mantelpiece, rereading a line of the codicil for the hundredth time. When the familiar ache knotted in his chest, he began pacing again, trying, unsuccessfully, to bury his thoughts in the bequest. But then the knock came again, quiet and uncertain. He snapped to attention.

"Come," he called, his heart beating erratically, knowing it would be Miss Woodridge but hoping it would be Phoebe.

The door cracked open. A small face peered in first — wide blue eyes beneath a mop of unruly curls — before a woman stepped forward and gently nudged the boy behind her skirts. Miss Woodridge and her son. Graeme puffed his cheeks and returned to his desk in long strides to welcome her.

"Beggin' your pardon, sir," she said, bobbing a shaky curtsy. "I... I weren't sure if I ought come back, sir, but seein' as how you said..."

"You are most welcome, Miss Woodridge. Please, come in."

Her hair was tucked beneath a faded straw hat, her gown patched but carefully mended. She snatched off the hat and clutched the brim in both hands so tightly her knuckles whitened. The boy pressed his cheek into her hip, trying to disappear behind her skirts. When she stepped inside, she did not approach the chair he gestured towards, rather hovered inside the doorway, twisting the hat.

"I'm glad you returned," Graeme coaxed, hoping to make her feel more welcome.

Her eyes darted around the study with the instinctive discomfort of a servant in a room not meant for her. He realized how desperate she must have been to come to him yesterday.

Her throat bobbed as she swallowed. "I hope I'm not makin' trouble for you, sir. I don't want no bother. Only I can't get work nowhere." She touched the boy's curls. "And I thought, like I said, maybe the new earl might give me a word, a proper reference, like. So folks won't think... won't think I were put out for—"

"Please, sit," he urged, interrupting.

She shook her head. "No, sir. No, thank you, but I wouldn't dare set myself in such a fine chair again."

Yes, she must have been awfully desperate yesterday, and curiously more hopeful than she was today.

He did not press her again to sit; rather, he took a gentler approach. "I have been thinking a great deal about what you told me yesterday."

"Aye, sir."

"There is something you must know, something that will affect your circumstances."

Her fingers twisted the brim of the hat. "Some-thin' wrong, sir?"

"No, but something unexpected."

She stiffened.

"The late Earl of Collumby made provisions for you. And for your son."

Miss Woodridge frowned. "Pro-visions, sir?"

"He left you something in his will. A... *substantial* inheritance."

Silence. A deep, hollow silence that threatened to swallow the room. She stared at him, stared hard, her eyes narrowing slightly, as though trying to interpret a dialect she had never heard.

"No, sir, that ain't... that can't be right."

"It is."

Shaking her head, she said, "I... sir, I never asked him for nothin'. I swear it on my soul. I never—" Her voice cracked. "I weren't his... bird. Please believe me."

Firmly but gently, Graeme said, "I believe you."

She burst into tears anyway. Nothing loud or dramatic. Silent, shuddering tremors of someone whose dignity had been worn thin.

Her son tugged at her gown. "Mama?"

"Hush, pet. Mama's all right." She wiped her face on her sleeve, cheeks flushing in mortification. "Sir, I can't be takin' money for... for what happened. I never meant to get in the family way. I never meant no harm. I only kept quiet 'cause I'd nowhere else to go, and he... he weren't cruel, not truly. He were lonely, I think. But I didn't... I didn't want wages for it. That ain't decent."

"This is not payment, Miss Woodridge. Nor charity. This is provision. Provision the earl chose to make, freely and deliberately. The codicil was properly witnessed. It is lawful, binding, and meant for your protection."

She shook her head again, more faintly now. "I don't understand, sir."

"Then allow me to explain." Carefully, precisely, he led her through the details, trying not to overwhelm her. "The earl set aside a living for you and the boy. Your son will never want for food or shelter. A small cottage, modest and manageable, where you and the boy may reside if you wish, along with any family; it is yours to do with as you choose. A sum has also been left, large enough that you will never need to beg for employment again. The sum will be put into a trust to protect the child's future, ensuring neither of you may be taken advantage of."

Miss Woodridge stared at him as if seeing a ghost. "A... a trust, sir?"

"Yes."

"For my lad?"

"Yes."

Slowly, she looked down, brushing her son's curls, hat still clutched in her other hand. "He'll be safe?"

"Safe and provided for, never wanting."

Her eyes watered. "Then... if it's for him... then... I'll accept, sir. He deserves better'n what I can give."

Graeme nodded. "I've sent word to the estate solicitor to return from London. He will help you finalize the details and provide instructions for what comes next."

She bobbed a jerky curtsy. "Thank you, sir. Bless you. I don't know what we done to deserve such kindness."

He did not say his next thought aloud: *This is not kindness. This is justice.*

Hugging her son close, she said, "I'll not trouble you longer, sir. I'll come back when you send for me. I don't want to be takin' no one's seat or food. We'll walk home."

"Nonsense." Before she could protest, Graeme tugged at the bellrope. Within moments, a footman appeared at the door. "Please have the carriage take Miss Woodridge wherever she needs."

"Oh no, sir," she squawked, looking from the footman to Graeme with panicked, wide eyes. "That's far too fine for the likes of—"

"It is my wish."

After studying his expression, she surrendered with another curtsy, picking up her son to balance on a hip, the straw hat flattened under her son's leg. "Thank you, sir, truly."

Once she left, Graeme sat at the desk and detailed the arrangements for Miss Woodridge to the estate solicitor. The cottage would be prepared for her arrival. The bulk of the funds would go into a managed trust, ensuring her son's inheritance was protected. From that trust, a yearly allowance would be paid directly to Miss Woodridge for living expenses, providing a manageable, regular income that would not overwhelm her or insult her dignity.

Details complete, he signed the paper, rolled the blotter, melted wax into a small, even circle, then reached for the signet ring in the drawer to apply the seal. Done.

In the distance, he could hear the carriage pulling away down the lane. The late earl, for all his faults, had made his own kind of amends. All the estate solicitor's worries that the mysterious Miss P.W. had schemed and plotted to bankrupt the estate for her own benefit had come to nothing more than a bitter, lonely man assuaging his guilt, or whatever motive had moved him to be generous in the end.

Ironic, he thought, that all the man had ever wanted was an heir, and yet when he finally realized that goal, he refused to humble himself to marry beneath him to legitimize the heir, only agreeing to marry below his station through the union with Phoebe Whittington, when he saw the end was near. Graeme had little pity for a man who, to the end, refused to acknowledge his brother's descendants, and although providing handsomely for his natural son—only from his deathbed—would still leave his bride-to-be abandoned in limbo.

Ah, Phoebe.

Where was Phoebe?

Did she intend to come back to him at all?

He walked over to the window overlooking the garden, hoping to catch a glimpse of her. The sky had darkened to pewter grey. He lowered his forehead to the windowpane. In the past two days, he had untangled every knot except the one that mattered most.

Chapter 21

The sky remained low and leaden when Graeme entered the estate chapel Sunday morning, a mirror to his mood. He took his place near the back, not out of irreverence, but because it would offer the best vantage to steal glances at the young woman who, until three days ago, had turned his world inside out.

The problem? Phoebe Whittington was not there.

Not in her pew.

Not in any pew.

Not even her maid in sight.

A prickle crawled up Graeme's spine. She had not missed chapel once since her arrival.

The chaplain began the service, voice steady, but Graeme heard none of it. Every hymn sounded distant, every prayer muffled. He tried, absurdly, to convince himself she must be unwell, perhaps fatigued or overset, anything to ignore the growing dread pooling, cold and heavy, in his chest.

When the final blessing was offered, Graeme rose first, impatient and afraid. He did not wait for anyone, did not think, only moved.

Out of the chapel. Through the gallery. Up the main staircase. Into the east wing. Straight to Phoebe's suite.

He knocked once.

No answer.

He tried the handle.

It yielded.

Her rooms were immaculate, curtains drawn back, nothing amiss except—and this struck him like a blow—the absence of *anything* resembling a guest in residence. No bonnets by the door, no shawls on the wall hooks, no feminine treasures on the table. A coldness gripped him.

"Miss Whittington?" he called, though he already knew she was not within. "Phoebe?"

No sound. No rustle. No trace of occupancy.

Then, his gaze snagged on something resting atop the dressing table: a folded sheet of cream paper.

It took long minutes for him to move towards it. His limbs dragged, as though wading against a current, one that threatened to sweep him away. When he lifted the note, the air *whooshed* from his lungs to see it not addressed to *Graeme*, rather *the Earl of Collumby*. His heartbeat pitched, hard and swift.

He opened the letter.

To the Earl of Collumby,

I relinquish all claim to the inheritance bequeathed to me in the codicil. I did not seek it. I do not desire it. I never have. I ask only that my name be removed from any record or rumor that might imply I profited from the late earl's death.

Whatever he intended by naming me in the codicil, I pray my refusal makes plain that I did not come to Shropshire as a fortune-hunter. I have known too well the ruin that comes when a gentleman's declarations are not what they seem. I will not repeat past mistakes.

I wish you and your household peace. My departure will spare all parties further scandal.

P.W.

His stomach dropped. She had signed with the initials she believed the late earl had used for her, those same initials she now thought he had used to purchase her, control her, and deceive her. She thought *he* had been Freddy all over again, that *Graeme* had been Freddy all over again.

He pressed the heels of his palms to his eyes, the truth detonating like a cannon blast. She *had* read the codicil, and she had seen everything from the perspective of the inheritance: his silence, his flirtation, his kiss, his confession. And she had come to the worst, most understandable, most devastating conclusion imaginable: *that he had seduced her for thirty thousand pounds and a cottage.*

His knees nearly buckled.

For longer than he could say, he could do nothing but stand there, breath coming in shallow heaves, letter shaking in his grip. He had feared she would choose money over love, feared she would retreat into her pride, even feared her independence might tempt her away from him, but he had never, not once, thought she might believe *he* had been the one scheming. In her eyes, he was a villain, a liar, and a deceiver.

Phoebe, hurt and humiliated once before, would naturally believe the worst. How had he not foreseen that?

"Oh, Phoebe." His voice cracked.

Leaning a hand against the wall, he forced himself to breathe, to think. When had she left? Friday? Saturday? How far could she have gone? He moved quickly, rifling through the wardrobe, through the dressing room, through the maid's chamber. All empty.

He rang the bell.

Within moments, a footman appeared, eyes widening at Graeme's expression.

"When was Miss Whittington last seen?" he demanded.

"Yesterday morning, sir. At first light. She and her maid were walking to Tansy Hollow."

Graeme's pulse spiked. "No carriage, then," he mumbled to himself.

"No, sir."

Of course not. Phoebe was too clever. She would not announce her departure, not when shame fueled her flight. She could have walked to Tansy Hollow, and then from there taken a cart to Upton Magna to catch the mail coach to London or hire a post-chaise. He knew the direction, regardless. The London road. She would be miles ahead by now.

"Yesterday, you say?"

"Yes, sir," confirmed the footman.

Yesterday's head start would be better than a Friday headstart. If she left yesterday morning, she would not be beyond reach.

Whatever coach she had chosen, assuming she did catch one, would have stopped overnight. It would not travel on a Sunday before the afternoon, at the earliest. He *could* overtake her. If he hurried.

He snapped upright. "Saddle a horse. Immediately."

The footman bolted.

Graeme folded the letter and slipped it into his coat pocket. He would go after her. He would find her. With urgency and a hammering pulse, he strode down the corridor. He would explain everything, the codicil, Penelope Woodridge, the truth of his silence on those points, the truth of his heart. And he would not rest, not for one mile or one hour, until he had her safely before him again. She was *not* lost to him, not yet. But if he did not act now, she soon would be.

Taking the steps two at a time, he rushed to his apartments to change into his riding habit as swiftly as he could, for there was not a minute to lose.

Only minutes later, but what felt like hours, he was outside and mounting in one fluid motion, even as the groom was still tightening the saddle straps.

"Which way, sir?" the groom called.

Gathering the reins, jaw set with fierce resolve. "London."

And he thundered down the drive, the wind slicing past him, their entire future riding on whether he caught her in time.

Chapter 22

Phoebe had not realized how loud the world was until she tried to run away from it. The carrier's cart rattled and jolted over every rut in the road, each bump knocking her spine and each creak complaining in a different key. The canvas hood snapped in the wind. Chickens in a wicker crate objected shrilly to their circumstances. Somewhere behind her, a pig grunted his steady disapproval of existence. None of it quite managed to drown out the sound of her own thoughts.

She bemoaned missing the mail coach.

Fanny sat beside her, bonnet brim pulled low, gloved fingers clenched tightly together. Their trunks sat wedged against the cart's side, rope biting into worn leather. On the opposite bench, an elderly gypsy with a shawl over her cap dozed with her chin on her chest, rosary beads dangled between gnarled fingers. Every now and then, the woman would snore, jolt awake, murmur a prayer, then drift off again.

The driver clicked his tongue, and the horse trudged on.

Fields stretched on either side of the narrow lane, pale green under a sky of high, thin clouds.

Hedgerows blurred by. Once, Phoebe would have admired the rolling West Midlands' hills, would have compared their soft rise and fall to the swell of music in a country dance or the fold of silk in a ball gown. Now, the landscape was simply distance. Distance between her and Lobelia Hall. Between her and a piece of parchment with her initials.

And most significant of all, between her and the man who had lied.

You have your dignity still, she reminded herself with hollow words. *You did not stay for the promise of money. You walked away.*

Fanny leaned in and whispered, "Are you quite comfortable, miss?"

Phoebe's lips curved into a brittle smile. "Perfectly. I've always dreamed of rattling to London in the company of poultry."

It had been Fanny who, after Phoebe had sobbed out everything the night before, had helped her fold gowns without asking questions she already knew the answers to, and Fanny who had arranged with the dairywoman's cousin for a place on the carrier's cart to the next posting town, where they hoped to catch a London coach. This was not Phoebe's first escape back to London, but it would certainly be her last. Mr. Vavara and India now awaited, a fitting consequence to her second round of misplaced trust and naivety; at least the merchant's intentions were honest, however undesirable.

Phoebe's throat ached, her mind returning, unbidden, to the letter she left on the dressing table, to the study, to... his earnest eyes, tender voice, and proposal for courtship. Then the codicil. Graeme had known and said nothing. He had kissed her while an enormous inheritance with her initials lay hidden in his study. She had told him about Freddy, about everything, and still he had thought it acceptable to hold such a secret from her.

Somewhere ahead, a lark ascended, singing as if the world were not a place where men lied with soft lips and hooded eyes.

The cart rounded a bend. The lane narrowed between steep banks, hedges high on either side. The horse slowed of its own accord on the incline, hooves thudding dully. The driver clucked encouragement.

Behind them, faint at first beneath the squeak and rattle of the cart, came another sound: distant, rhythmic thunder.

Hoofbeats.

Phoebe's heart gave a perfidious flutter. Riders used the main coaching roads often, she told herself. This was nothing. A farmer. A messenger, perhaps.

The hoofbeats grew louder, faster, gaining on them. She refused to turn around. She refused to crane about like some heroine in a lurid Minerva Press novel, ears pricked for the sound of a lover's pursuit.

Fanny, less lofty in her resolutions, twisted to peer out the back of the canvas curtain. "There's a rider coming up quick, miss."

"Then he will pass us," Phoebe snipped, keeping her gaze fixed firmly ahead. "The road does not belong to us alone."

The horse panted now, straining against the weight of cart and passengers. All the while, the hoofbeats drew nearer, then shifted rhythm, slowing, and drawing alongside.

The cart driver pulled at the reins. "Steady now, steady."

A man's voice, breathless and dreadfully familiar, cut through the clatter. "Ho there! Driver, might I beg a word?"

Phoebe's heart stopped.

This was impossible. Absolutely impossible!

She stared hard at the opposite hedge.

The cart lurched to a hesitant halt. The chickens protested. The old woman jolted awake with an indignant snort.

Fanny hissed, "Miss—"

"Don't. Do *not* say his—"

"Miss Whittington?" came that same voice, nearer now, closer than her own pulse. "Phoebe?"

Her resolve shattered with one treacherous movement: she turned.

Graeme sat astride a lathered bay, hatless, hair wind-tossed, coat flung back, dust streaking his boots. His cravat was askew in a way that would have sent any London valet into hysterics. His chest rose and fell with the effort of hard riding. His eyes—those dear, infuriating, earnest eyes—were fixed entirely on her.

Phoebe's breath caught. For the span of one heartbeat, pure relief washed through her, as fierce as it was foolish. Then memory returned like a slap: the codicil, the secrecy, the humiliation. She straightened her spine.

"Mr. Ellison," she said coolly. "You are a long way from your ledgers."

He flinched. "May I beg a moment of your time," he said, voice rough, "if only at the roadside?"

The driver shifted uncertainly on his box. "Beggin' your pardon, sir, but the lady's fare is paid to the next town. I can't be stoppin' long."

"I will compensate you for any delay," Graeme said without taking his gaze off Phoebe. "Handsomely."

The driver brightened. "No objection from me, sir. The lady?"

Every eye in the cart turned to her: Fanny's anxious, the elderly woman's curious, the chickens' beady and indifferent. Phoebe's fingers tightened into a fist. She could refuse. She should refuse. She had written what needed to be said. She owed *him* nothing more.

But, maddeningly, she remembered the sound of his voice when he had said, *I believe you*. The way he had looked at her in the portrait gallery. The gentleness of his hands when he had held her as if she were something precious. Perhaps she owed herself at least one answer. Yes, this was for her, not for him. She owed him nothing.

"Very well," she said, keeping her tone thin with dignity. "A moment."

The driver clicked his tongue, guiding the cart to the verge until the wheel bumped against the bank. Graeme swung out of the saddle, wincing as his boots hit the ground. Holding the reins in one hand, he used the other to steady the horse's neck.

Fanny leaned in again. "I'll come down with you, miss."

"No. Wait here. If I am foolish enough to swoon into the ditch, you may fetch me then."

Phoebe gathered her skirts and stepped down from the cart, accepting the driver's hand for balance but jerking away before Graeme could offer his. The lane smelled of dust and trampled grass and horse sweat. They stood a few paces apart beside the cart's wheel, the horse shifting restlessly at Graeme's shoulder. The driver made a show of checking harness straps while obviously listening with both ears.

Graeme swallowed audibly. Up close, he looked worse than she had first thought. There was stubble on his jaw, dark circles beneath his eyes, and the strained tightness around his mouth of a man who had been fretful for longer than he cared to admit.

"I did not expect to find you… on a cart," he said inanely.

Phoebe arched a brow. "My apologies. Next time I flee a household, I shall be sure to hire a gilded carriage, that I may better suit your sensibilities."

A breath of startled laughter escaped him. "Phoebe—"

"You have had two days to speak to me in person," she cut in, the hurt sharpening her words. "Instead, you let me sit alone and think while you… what? Balanced accounts? Wrote to more marquesses to pry into my life? I confess the romance of it all overwhelmed me."

He drew in a breath. "I did not come sooner because I thought you were… choosing. Between the codicil and—" He faltered, then, "—and me."

She stared at him, speechless for a moment. "You thought I was up in my room weighing a fortune against a clerk? How *flattering*."

He grimaced. "I know how it sounds. Abominable. But also know what the codicil would mean to most, and I… I could not fault you if you wished to be free."

He said the last word, *free*, with such aching sincerity that for a heartbeat her anger waned. Then she remembered the codicil.

"You speak of my freedom, yet you had the power to change my whole life in a stroke of your quill, and you said nothing. *Nothing*, Mr. Ellison. You kept your silence even as you kissed me." Her voice thinned. "You let me believe your regard for me was untainted by… by avarice, when all the while you had a reason to treat me with such tenderness."

"Phoebe, no. No." He reached into his coat, hands fumbling, and pulled out folded paper. "I found your letter. I know what you believe, what you fear — that I am another Freddy, that I courted you for the sake of the codicil. You wrote — "

Her face flamed in rage and embarrassment. "You had no right to read that. It was not addressed to you."

Pocketing the letter, he said quietly, "But it *was* addressed to me. Or rather, to the Earl of Collumby, which, in this unfortunate instance, amounts to the same person."

She blinked. "I addressed it to the *earl*, not to *you*."

His mouth twitched with rueful humor. "Yes, well. I am both."

Silence fell, thick as fog.

"You are *what*?" she asked at last.

Cringing, he said, "I had hoped to unfold this part more delicately."

"Try," she suggested, feeling faintly lightheaded. "Begin with how the humble clerk who kissed me in a portrait gallery has suddenly become an earl in a dusty lane."

"The humble clerk who kissed you in a portrait gallery was always an earl," he said. "An earl in disguise." Seeing her expression, he added hastily, "Not to mock you. Not to toy with you. I swear it. I came to Lobelia Hall as Mr. Ellison because I needed to know what kind of man my great-uncle had been, what kind of life he had led, what dangers and obligations I would inherit. I needed to see the estate through unvarnished eyes. The staff would not speak freely to an earl, but they would to a solicitor."

"Good heavens," Phoebe whispered, her knees feeling oddly unreliable. "All this time…?"

"All this time I have been Graeme Lockwood," he admitted. "Now the Earl of Collumby. And all this time, you have been the only person who spoke to me as if I were a man, not a tradesman, not a solicitor, not an earl, merely a man."

"Merely a man who *lied* about his name, his position, and an enormous inheritance with my initials on it," she said tartly, clinging to indignation as the only solid ground.

"Yes," he said hoarsely. "And I am trying, badly, I admit, to explain why. May I?"

She folded her arms. "You have ridden me down in the middle of a public road. I suppose I cannot stop you from speaking."

From his perch, the carrier cleared his throat pointedly. "If you're goin' to be long, sir, I'll just see to the horse's nosebag, shall I?"

"Please," Graeme said with a nod.

The driver hopped down and led the horse a few paces off to a patch of grass, giving them his back and the pretense of privacy.

Graeme turned back to Phoebe. Dust streaked his cheekbone. Without thinking, she *almost* reached up to swipe it away with her fingertips. Instead, she tucked her hands firmly under her arms.

"I should have told you about the codicil sooner," he said. "That is the heart of it. I did not because I was a coward and a fool. At first, I believed you were the Miss P.W. my great-uncle mentioned. You arrived within days of my learning of the legacy. You were of the right disposition, the right initials, the right circumstances. But then, you told me about Freddy, about Scotland, about the surprise of the renewed proposal. The pieces did not fit so well anymore."

"They fit well enough that you thought I meant to bankrupt the estate," she snapped.

"I did. For about a day. But then I read the journals, the letters… I saw the way he wrote, the way he thought. I watched *you*. You did not scheme or cajole. You did not so much as *hint* about money. You were simply… yourself. Bold. Frightened. Trying not to be. The more I observed, the more certain I became that you were not what he had imagined you to be." His voice lowered. "And the more certain I became that you were far better."

Heat prickled at the corners of her eyes. She blinked away angrily. "That does not excuse—"

"It does not," he agreed. "I told myself I would speak to the housekeeper and the chaplain first, confirm Miss P.W.'s identity before I turned your life upside down. But then… well, you rode with me, and painted with me, and laughed in my arms. I… I forgot everything but the feel of you against me. I liked being myself with you, not a man who had to tell you the worst news of your life, that there was an inheritance that *might* be yours, but might not be, that *could* free you if you were the correct P.W., but that could have you lose the chance at *more* if you thought independence a better option."

"The worst news of my life," she repeated, stunned. "You thought telling me there was a fortune in my name would be the *worst* news of my life?"

"I thought that telling you *too soon* might turn what we had into a transaction. I wanted… selfishly, perhaps unforgivably… more time with you where nothing hung between us except our own choices. I wanted you to have the freedom of liking me, or not, without weighing me against a codicil." A humorless smile tugged his lips. "And then I kissed you, and any hope of behaving prudently deserted me."

She swallowed. The memory of that kiss reverberated through her like the echo of a ringing bell.

"You told me about Freddy, about a gentleman who claimed he loved you when what he wanted was your money. That he courted you not for yourself but for your dowry. You *trusted* me with that. And still, when you saw the codicil, you believed I had done the same."

"What else was I to think?" she demanded, voice cracking. "You hid it from me. You let me sit in your study and work beside you while a fortune sat on your desk — with my initials on it! You allowed me to talk about my lack of dowry, about my fears, about my desire simply to be wanted, and you said nothing. And then you offered me courtship." Her throat tightened. "How was I to distinguish between your regard and your calculation?"

His shoulders sagged. "By the one fact I never thought I would have to state aloud. I never needed a penny of that money."

She stared at him. "No one is so wealthy they would not notice thirty thousand pounds, sir."

"Perhaps not many," he said. "But a man whose grandfather built a flourishing trade, whose father doubled it, and who has spent his adult life growing it further, notices a great deal less than most. The Lockwood warehouses do not vanish because one codicil moves an unentailed sum from an estate. Nor do the investments my father and I have made. The rents of Lobelia Hall matter. The livelihoods of those who depend on it matter. Thirty thousand pounds is only ruinous to *them* if I refuse to shoulder the loss, but luckily for us all, it is a small amount to my coffers."

The number hit her at last. "Thirty… thousand…"

"Yes. He meant it to wound the cut-off branch of the family, I think. To punish them by bleeding the estate dry. And, in his twisted way, to keep his natural son from want." He drew a breath. "The codicil was not written for you, Phoebe. It was written for Penelope Woodridge. The maid he seduced but never married. The woman he cast off, believing the codicil would pay his sins."

She could not seem to find her breath. "Penelope, not Phoebe," she repeated.

"She came to the Hall," he explained. "Begging only for a reference, terrified anyone should think she had tempted him. She did not even know he had left her anything. The housekeeper dismissed her out of shame. The chaplain assumed someone had informed the solicitor. And the solicitor assumed Miss P.W.

would arrive waving demands for an inheritance. Instead, *you* arrived. A different P.W., with different troubles, and with an almost-betrothal. And I, idiot that I am, mistook you for the first." He dragged his hand down his face. "I have now set matters right. The codicil is being executed as it should have been from the first. The cottage and the trust are hers and her son's."

Phoebe's head spun. The road tilted. She put a hand out, instinctively, steadying herself against Graeme's arm. He cupped her elbow, his hand firm and warm.

"So, I never…" She could not finish.

"You were never named. Which means I failed you in two ways at once. I suspected you of scheming for an inheritance that was not yours, and when I realized my mistake, I did not tell you for fear of losing the time with you I had come to treasure."

She stared at his waistcoat, faint, confused, unsure how to respond.

"You said in your letter you relinquished any claim to the codicil, wished only to remove yourself so the estate would not suffer further." His voice roughened. "Is it foolish for me to believe you had begun to care for me, that you might still care, might still hope?"

She did not answer. Heat surged to her cheeks.

He stepped closer, cautiously, as if approaching a skittish horse. "You are not a fortune huntress. You never were. Every doubt I had was my flaw, not your fault. You trusted me first, but I failed to trust you in return. That is on my conscience, not yours. But if you walk away now believing that I ever courted you for money, I could not bear it."

She gasped for air, then bitterly spat out, "Why *did* you court me, then, *my lord*?"

"For your laugh," he said without hesitation. "For the way you argue when you are frightened. For your ridiculous courage. For the way you looked at me when you thought I was only a clerk and still made me feel like a man worth looking at. I wish I could tell you it was love from the first, but it wasn't. It was irritation, then reluctant admiration, then an affection that grew every time you walked into a room."

He clasped her hand and held it to his heart. She did not pull away.

"I am not asking you to believe in love all at once," he said. "Only to consider that perhaps what stands between us is not greed, but my spectacular talent for mishandling the truth."

Against her will, a strangled sound escaped her lips, half laugh and half sob. "You are the worst suitor I have ever had," she managed.

"I would be more offended," he said, eyes glinting, "If I did not know the competition includes Freddy."

A laugh burst from her, shocked and tearful. She clapped her free hand over her mouth, appalled at herself, but it was too late. The sound was out, hanging in the air like birdsong.

Graeme's shoulders eased a fraction.

"You chased down a carrier's cart on the Sabbath," she said, lowering her hand. "You flew down the road like a madman just to argue with me in the dust."

He glanced at his horse. "He and I are of one mind on the madness. But yes, I did."

She looked at him for a long, searching moment. Dust. Stubble. Rumpled cravat. Raw apology in every line of him. "And what do you want now?"

"A chance," he answered simply. "Only that. A chance to return to Lobelia Hall *together*. A chance to show you, overtly and honestly, what my feelings are and how I intend to act on them. A chance to court you properly, openly, as the man I am, not the solicitor I pretend to be. If, at any time, you decide I am not worth the trouble, you may leave with all my blessing and half my fortune besides, and I will not stop you." His mouth quirked. "But I would rather like the opportunity to convince you I am."

She balked. "Half your for—"

"Hyperbole," he hastened to clarify. "Mostly. I would prefer not to test the accounts *that* far. The point remains: you do not need my title or my money to make your choice. You never did."

Her heart took a particularly reckless leap. "And what would people say if they learned their dignified new earl chased a woman down the London road to beg her to come home?"

He shrugged. "They may say what they please. But perhaps," and this he added with a spark in his eyes, "some of them might say that for once, a Collumby chose well."

Silence stretched between them, but it had changed, no longer a wall, rather a held breath. Phoebe looked backed at the cart. Fanny watched, twisting the ribbon of her bonnet. The gypsy peered unabashedly over the top of her shawl, eyes twinkling with scandalized delight. The driver pretended to adjust the harness again, failing utterly to conceal his grin.

Turning back to Graeme, Phoebe said, "I left because I believed you had chosen money over me. Because I believed you had used your position and knowledge to... to play with my heart. I could not bear it if that were true."

"It is not."

"I know." The realization had slid into her heart somewhere in his rambling and breathless confession. "You are a fool. And a coward. And very likely the worst liar I have ever met."

"Agreed."

"And I..." her voice trembled. "I am terrified of loving anyone again."

"I know."

She took a deep breath, inviting the air to fill her lungs, cool and sharp. She thought of Lobelia Hall, of its gallery, its garden, the linden tree, even of a stranger's son, safe now with a provision and cottage... of the staff who had begun to treat her not as an intrusion but as someone who belonged... of the way Graeme had watched her walk through the garden, his gaze warmer than sunlight.

"The road goes two ways," she said at last. "Towards London. And back to Lobelia Hall."

He nodded, squeezing her hand.

"If I return with you, you must promise there will be no more disguises, no secret inheritances, no eavesdropping behind the Ficus in the conservatory."

He stared at her blankly. "I have never hidden behind a —"

"Hyperbole," she teased, rather enjoying his ears turning a faint pink. "You must promise that if your fear whispers something dreadful about me in your head, you will not believe it until you have asked me first."

"I swear."

"And," she added, "you must be prepared that I will likely fall in love with you. And I shall be very cross if you make me regret it."

Something in his face crumpled and smoothed at once, as if relief had buckled him from the inside. He stepped closer still, lifting her hand against his lips, his fingers shaking slightly.

"Then," he said huskily, "I will devote myself to never giving you cause to be cross. Or at least, not on that subject. I will, of course, still argue with you about everything else. It would be a dull marriage otherwise."

The word hung between them—marriage—as startling as a dropped coin.

"Oh," she said.

"Too soon. Consider it… future ambition. For now, shall we begin with the ride back?"

He turned, beckoning to the driver. "How do you feel about exchanging your passengers for my horse?" he called. "I suspect the lady would prefer to finish her journey in a somewhat more comfortable vehicle."

The driver scratched his head. "Depends how comfortable your purse is feelin'."

Graeme glanced at Phoebe. "May I demonstrate that I do not, in fact, need yours or anyone else's money?"

She tossed her gaze to the sky, but said, "Very well. Buy the horse, the cart, the chickens, and the old woman's rosary while you are about it. Then, perhaps, I shall believe you."

His laughter spilled into the lane. He lifted her hand once more to his lips, pressing a kiss against her knuckles, reverent and shaken.

"Phoebe Whittington, you are everything I never knew I wanted. Come home with me?"

Her heart, the foolish thing, had already gone galloping after him hours ago. Catching up to it seemed the only sensible course left.

"Yes," she said. "Let us go home."

Epilogue

One Month Later

The carriage crested the rise overlooking Lobelia Hall just as the sun slipped past the western
hills, gilding every window in molten gold.
The old manor appeared to glow from within, as
though awakening to the new life Graeme Lockwood
and his family would breathe into it.

Graeme adjusted his starched shirt points with
the mild irritation of a man not yet accustomed to
tailoring that cost more than his entire tradesman's
wardrobe. The deep navy superfine suited him well —
too well, Phoebe had voiced more than once with a
tease of her eyelashes — and the silver-thread embroidery along his waistcoat made him look, and feel,
every inch the Earl of Collumby.

"It is utterly unfair that you look more handsome
in a few hours as an earl," Phoebe said, trying, and
failing, not to grin, "than you ever did in all the weeks
you spent pretending to be a solicitor."

"I'll have you know," Graeme replied, tapping his
signet ring, "my clerk attire was the height of modest
practicality. Very respectable. Very dignified."

"And very drab."

He chuckled.

Across from them, his mother dabbed at the corners of her eyes with her handkerchief. "You look splendid, my dears. Both of you. I still cannot believe it — my son, an earl, and me with a daughter-in-law to be!" She sighed. "I wish your father could be here for the turn of events. He never did have the opportunity to see the ancestral family home."

Graeme's sister, Harriet, leaned towards Phoebe conspiratorially. "He's been rehearsing with his ring all morning. I think he believes it gives him gravitas."

Phoebe chortled, obviously delighted at the visual of Graeme twisting, tapping, and flashing the ring in a variety of aristocratic poses.

Next to Graeme, a bespectacled gentleman cleared his throat.

Mr. Brant Ellison, the *real* Mr. Ellison, folded his hands primly over his leather folio. "For the record," he drawled, "I frown on theatrics. Case in point, I would like it known, I never push up my spectacles every third sentence as though they were attached to a spring."

"I would claim artistic liberties," Graeme defended, "but I truly do need spectacles to read, and I never accustomed to the snugger frames."

Phoebe snorted. "I found him convincing, Mr. Ellison. Uncanny resemblance to a solicitor. Never would have suspected otherwise."

"You missed your calling for the stage, Graeme," Harriet said with a titter.

"I demand a full accounting of what he got up to playing me," Mr. Ellison complained nasally. "My reputation may never recover if he played me poorly."

Trying not to laugh outright, Phoebe said to Graeme, "I warned you that someday you would have to answer to the man whose name you borrowed."

"And now I have. He shows no mercy," he said solemnly.

The carriage slowed as they reached the final curve of the drive. Below, the household staff gathered in neat rows, the butler at their head, the housekeeper beside him, all standing straight-backed and visibly tense with anticipation to meet the long-awaited new Earl of Collumby, accompanied by the earl's family, the earl's betrothed, and the familiar Mr. Ellison.

Fluttering with excitement, Phoebe whispered for his ears only, "Do you think they'll recognize you?"

"Not a chance. The tailoring and pomade have made me a different man entirely. Besides, they never looked past my spectacles."

Smirking, she pressed, "Care to place a wager on that?"

"I thought you'd never ask."

The carriage rolled to a stop.

When the door opened, and Graeme and Phoebe descended, the butler stepped forward and bowed with flawless dignity. If the man was shocked to see the former solicitor emerge from the carriage in full aristocratic splendor, he hid it expertly.

Graeme's gaze swept the staff in search of reactions as the *real* Mr. Ellison descended next before offering Harriet and Wilhemina a hand.

The butler bowed again, this time to Brant Ellison, and said, "Welcome back, Mr. Ellison. A pleasure to see you again."

Graeme murmured to his solicitor, "Your reputation precedes you after all."

Mr. Ellison puffed out his chest.

Behind the butler, he could see Mrs. Redshaw's lips pressed together. He could not read her expression.

Leaning close to Phoebe, he said, "They're fooled."

Phoebe shook her head almost imperceptibly. "On the contrary. *They know.*"

"Preposterous."

"They're only pretending."

"You're just greedy to win the wager," he teased. "Fortune huntress that you are."

Moving her lips within inches of his ear, she whispered, "You may pay whatever forfeit you choose."

He hoped his face did not flush for all to see.

Mrs. Redshaw stepped forward, curtsying deeply. "My lord. Welcome home to Lobelia Hall."

Unexpectedly, his heart gave a joyful leap. *Home.* From the way Phoebe squeezed his arm, he knew her joy ran far deeper. Her fingers curled around his sleeve as he guided her forward, ascending the front steps, the staff parting like a tide.

As they crossed the threshold into the great hall, Graeme bent his head. "Are you ready, my darling?"

"For what?"

"Everything. This house. This life. My family. Our family. Our future."

She rose on tiptoe and kissed him, light as a promise. "I want everything, but mostly you."

Behind them, a murmur rippled through the staff.

When he turned to welcome his mother and sister into the great hall for the grand welcome to their new home, he heard the housekeeper mutter to the butler, just loud enough for him to catch in the breeze: "I knew that clerk weren't a clerk."

A Note from the Author

Dear Reader,

Thank you for purchasing and reading this book. If you're interested in exploring some of the research that went into this book and others, do check out my research blog: https://www.paullettgolden.com/bookresearch

Supporting indie writers who brave self-publishing is important and appreciated. I hope you'll continue reading my novels, as I have many more titles to come.

I humbly request you review this book on Amazon with an honest opinion. Reviewing elsewhere is additionally much appreciated.

One way to support writers you've enjoyed reading, indie or otherwise, is to share their work with friends, family, book clubs, etc. Lend books, share books, exchange books, recommend books, and gift books. If you especially enjoyed a writer's book, lend it to someone to read in case they might find a new favorite author in the book you've shared.

Connect with me online at www.paullettgolden.com, or @paullettgolden on Instagram, Facebook, X, and Patreon, as well as Amazon's Author Central, Goodreads, BookBub, and LibraryThing.

All the best,
Paullett Golden

About the Author

Celebrated for her complex characters, realistic conflicts, and sensual portrayal of love, Paullett Golden writes historical romance for intellectuals. Her novels, set primarily in Georgian England, challenge the genre's norm by starring characters loved for their imperfections and idiosyncrasies. The writing aims for historical immersion into the social mores and nuances of Georgian England. Her plots explore human psyche, mental and physical trauma, and personal convictions. Her stories show love overcoming adversity. Whatever our self-doubts, *love will out*.

Paullett Golden completed her post-graduate work at King's College London, studying Classic British Literature. Her Ph.D. is in Composition and Rhetoric, her M.A. in British Literature from the

Enlightenment through the Victorian era, and her B.A. in English. Her specializations include creative writing and professional writing. She has served as a University Professor for nearly three decades and is a seasoned keynote speaker, commencement speaker, conference presenter, workshop facilitator, and writing retreat facilitator.

As an ovarian cancer survivor, she makes each day count, enjoying an active lifestyle of Spartan racing, powerlifting, hiking, antique car restoration, drag racing, butterfly gardening, competitive shooting, and gaming. Her greatest writing inspirations, and the reasons she chose to write in the clean historical romance genre, are Jane Austen, Charlotte Brontë, and Elizabeth Gaskell.

Connect online

paullettgolden.com
patreon.com/paullettgolden
instagram.com/paullettgolden
facebook.com/paullettgolden
x.com/paullettgolden